The Magic Chanter

Sheila Douglas

illustrated by Vikki Petrie

SCOTTISH CHILDREN'S PRESS

First published in 1997 by

SCOTTISH CHILDREN'S PRESS

Unit 14, Leith Walk Business Centre,
130 Leith Walk, Edinburgh EH6 5DT
Tel: 0131 555 5950 • Fax: 0131 555 5018
e-mail: scp@sol.co.uk

British Library Cataloguing in Publication Data
A catalogue record for this book is available from the British Library

The publisher acknowledges subsidy from the Scottish Arts Council
towards the publication of this volume

ISBN: 1 899827 10 2

Printed and bound by Redwood Books, Trowbridge, Wiltshire

Contents

1

The Gift

It all began one night when nine-year-old Iain Barlass was curled up in his pyjamas on his bedroom window-sill. He looked out on to the South Inch; a big green park with massive trees and lots of room to play football. Knowing his mother imagined him to be fast asleep, Iain shifted slightly on the sill and settled down to read as long as it was light. In May, this was for quite a while, and he was fairly enjoying *The Secret of the Black Tower* along with a bag of smuggled sweets. Everything was quiet except for the sound of the occasional car passing in the street below, and the faint voice of the television in the living-room.

Iain's dog, Bitsy, snuggled in beside him and snored quietly. He was called Bitsy because he was made up of 'bits o this an bits o that', a feeble joke that Iain's father would inflict on anyone who asked. A shaggy, multi-coloured dog, with a long head, short tail and high-pitched bark that always sounded excited, Bitsy was always at Iain's heel when he ran across the Inch, as he did most days after school, to the swings or the boating pond, or to kick a ball about with his pals. His mum called Bitsy Iain's bodyguard and she wasn't far wrong. More than once the alert dog had caught Iain's jeans in his teeth to stop him from running out in front of a car in his hurry to cross the street.

Iain clutched affectionately at Bitsy's thick coat as he read, but was surprised when the dog suddenly cringed and growled. At the same time a chill air seemed to seep in through the gaps in the window frame, making him shiver. He lifted his eyes from his book. His room had taken on quite a different look. Instead of his pine bed with its blue and white downie, his wardrobe and chest of drawers, bookshelf and toy box, there was a funny old high bed hung round with curtains, a huge dark-coloured wardrobe with mirrors on it and other heavy pieces of furniture Iain hadn't seen before. As he stared, terrified, a pale-faced lady glided in through the door and stopped before the wardrobe mirror. She was wearing a long, silvery grey dress, her fair hair hung in ringlets, tied with yellow ribbons and she was carrying a lacy white shawl. Strangest of all, she seemed to be floating above the floor.

Iain stared and stared for the longest time. There was a funny smell in the air, a kind of river smell and Iain noticed that she appeared to be dripping wet. Had she fallen in the river? The strange woman arranged her hair and smoothed her dress. Then with a long, deep sigh she drew the lacy shawl round her shoulders and turned in Iain's direction.

Scared she would see him, Iain clasped Bitsy tightly round the neck. The dog burst into excited barking, whereupon the lady vanished and the room became familiar once more. Iain dived into his bed, pulling the downie over his head, and Bitsy pushed in beside him, whimpering softly. 'What a feartie you are, Bitsy!' Iain whispered. The dog only nuzzled him hard as if to say, 'You're one to talk!'

The bedroom door opened and Iain's mother came in. 'What's all this carry-on?' she demanded, pretending to be angry. She switched on the light and pulled back the downie. 'Now, Iain, I told you not to play with Bitsy after bedtime!'

'Oh Mum!' Iain's voice quavered in spite of himself.

'What's wrong?'

'The room – it was all funny – and there was a lady . . . '

She gave him a hug. 'You've had a dream!' she laughed.

'No, no, Mum! I was awake.' Iain sat up in bed, anxious to convince her. 'I was on the window-sill reading – there's my book on the floor. Then Bitsy growled and I felt cold, and . . . and the room was all different. The bed had curtains. And there was a big wardrobe with a mirror. And a lady in a long dress appeared and she wasn't touching the floor and there was a damp smell.'

His mum laughed again. 'What an imagination you've got!'

'No,' Iain protested. 'How could I imagine it? I've never seen a bed like that. Or a wardrobe. Or a lady in a long dress.'

But his mother would not be persuaded. She sat down on his bed and stroked his hair in the way that made him grit his teeth – he wasn't a baby! 'You must've seen pictures,' she said, 'in books.'

'No I haven't,' he said, dodging away from her stroking hand. 'What pictures?'

'Pictures from long ago,' she said.

'Long ago?' he echoed.

'You're turning into a parrot,' she teased. 'Come on, now. Everything's all right. It's time you were asleep.' She pulled the downie over him, put out the light and closed the door.

Iain lay repeating over and over again, 'Long ago, long ago'. He sat up with jerk. 'That's it! I saw the room the way it was long ago.' The wonder of it almost took his breath away, but at the same time it seemed perfectly natural. He was both delighted and frightened. It was like standing at the top of Kinnoull Hill and looking over the edge of the cliff. 'Oh, Bitsy,' he whispered into the warm, breathing darkness at the foot of the bed, 'what a secret we've got now!'

If anything extra special happened to Iain or his friend, Neil Fraser, they would tell each other about it in school in a hidey-hole behind the dining hall. Neil was always inclined to scoff at anything he thought too far-fetched. He was a thin, dark-haired boy with glasses, and was nicknamed 'Sobersides' because he stayed serious-looking even when he was enjoying a joke. Iain and Neil both liked the same things – football, mystery stories and vanilla fudge. Neil was always having special adventures when his father took him fishing, or when he visited his uncle's farm. Iain was quite envious and felt his own special adventures, which were mainly to do with sight-seeing in Glasgow or Edinburgh, were dull by comparison. He had seen sky-diving at Scone Aerodrome, when Neil had been laid up with mumps, which made up for a lot, and he had seen the Isle of Skye Hotel burn down. But somehow he felt that if he told Neil about the grey lady and the transformed bedroom, he just wouldn't swallow it. 'I wonder what'll happen next,' Iain thought.

For a long time, nothing did. After a while Iain began to think his mum had been right and he'd dreamt it all. Then one Saturday he had to go with her to meet a friend for lunch in the Granary Restaurant. Iain wasn't looking forward to it one bit – they were bound to talk endlessly about boring things he didn't understand, like weddings and operations. But of course he didn't mind the chicken and chips and trifle he was allowed to have.

'Why's it called the Granary?' he asked and his mum told him it had once been a grain store. He was thinking about this as he went to the toilet. He didn't really need the toilet, but it was a good excuse to have a wander through the restaurant, which was an old building. It had bare dark stone walls which made Iain think of an old castle, and there were heavy curtains and wrought iron screens that gave the place a medieval appearance, or at least were meant to do. It didn't really surprise him when he came round a corner and found a man in a long dark robe sitting at a desk writing. His pen seemed to be made out of a feather, which he dipped into a bottle of dark fluid every now and then.

'That's funny,' thought Iain. 'Gran once told me that when she was a wee girl at school, they used pen and ink. But nobody does that now. Perhaps they've just put him here to look like someone from long ago.' Iain crept up beside the man, who was scratching with his pen and muttering what were probably rude words because it wouldn't work properly. Iain tried to see what he was writing. It seemed to be some kind of list, with numbers in it.

The man had a bald head, with a fringe of grey hair round it, and there was something hanging from the cord round his waist.

Bending down to peer closely at it, Iain saw it was a long string of amber-coloured beads with a wooden cross on it. The paper he was writing on was coarse and brownish and Iain could just make out the last entry, which said: 'Ber meal – 3 Bolls.'

Just then the man laid down his pen and took the string of beads into his hand, letting them slip through his fingers one by one. His lips moved and Iain strained his ears to hear what he was saying. He caught what sounded like 'No bees,' then a tug on his arm made him turn his head.

'Come on, Iain,' said his mother's voice. 'We're going home now. I thought we'd lost you.'

'I was just watching the old man,' said Iain.

'What old man?'

When he looked, the old man was no longer there, just a table with a vase of flowers on it. 'He's gone now,' said Iain, 'but he was here. He was sitting at a table writing.'

'You've still got a bit of trifle on your chin,' said his mum, handing him a tissue. 'Come on now.'

As he followed her out of the restaurant, his head was buzzing with all the questions he wanted to ask. What was ber meal? What did the man mean by 'no bees'? Who was he? What was he? Why was he wearing a black robe? Why was he using an old pen? On the way home he tried asking his mum, but she didn't pay much attention and simply said, 'I've no idea,' and tugged his hair teasingly. But Iain knew that once again he had seen something from long ago. He must have a gift of being able to see such things. Why and how this could be, he hadn't a clue. He told Bitsy about the old man when he got home. When he talked to Bitsy, it was always reassuring, because the dog would sit looking straight into his eyes with an expression that plainly said, 'I believe you.' Iain knew fine that no one else would.

'I must find out who that old man was,' Iain said, as he bounced a ball for Bitsy to fetch. 'I must.' Bitsy came and nuzzled his knees as if to say, 'I'm with you.'

A day or two later, in school, his teacher Mr McFatridge gave out a new history book to the class. Iain thought that Mr McFatridge – nicknamed Fattie, although he wasn't – was not bad as teachers go. He was certainly an improvement on the teacher he'd had the year before, who shouted and was always punishing people. Fattie was quite strict but he never shouted, and he gave rewards rather than punishments. No one was frightened to talk to him and sometimes he said things that were quite funny. When Iain opened the new history book, he saw something that made him gasp out loud.

'What's the matter, Iain?' asked Fattie.

'That picture!' Iain almost shouted. 'It's just like the man I saw in the Granary.'

'Well, don't deafen us all!' said Fattie, coming over to Iain's desk and looking at the page. 'That's a Carthusian Monk,' he said.

'What's that?' asked Iain.

'They were an order of monks. In fact, they still are. I'll be telling you all about them in the lessons we're going to have.'

Iain sighed; history wasn't his favourite subject. But then a thought struck him. 'Were there ever any Car-thingmybobs in Perth?'

'Oh yes indeed,' said Fattie. 'It's the history of Perth we're going to be finding out about.'

'I saw a man just like that in the Granary,' Iain told him.

'Well, as I said, there still are Carthusian monks, even today.'

'Oh, but he was from long ago,' said Iain. 'He was sitting writing with a feather pen.'

'A quill?' said Mr McFatridge. 'Was this some kind of tableau?'

'What's that?'

'A kind of scene set up; a staged thing.'

'Maybe it was. He wrote "Ber meal – 3 bolls". Then he was – I don't know – counting his beads and he was kind of muttering. All I heard was "No bees", then my mother came and he was away.'

The teacher looked down at him with a slightly puzzled look. 'What's this you're telling me? Aren't you getting mixed up with something you saw on TV?'

'No! It's true! I saw him!' said Iain.

Mr McFatridge just smiled and said nothing. The history lesson began and he started to explain some of the things in the first chapter of the book. Iain had always thought history was dead boring. He'd never bothered to listen much but just sat and day-dreamed about the games he'd play with Neil and Bitsy on the Inch after school. But this was different because he had seen a real man in a long robe who wrote 'Ber meal' and said 'No bees'.

He looked back at the book to see what it called him. A Carsuthian was it? No, a Carthusian, whatever that meant. There had been a few monasteries in Perth at one time, it seemed, and one of them was Blackfriars Monastery. It had stood near where Blackfriars Street was now. 'That's not far from the North Inch, near where Gran and Grandpa stay,' he thought.

'Look at page four,' said Fattie. 'There's a drawing that shows a plan of a monastery. It's not any particular one, just something like it. See, there's a place where the monks prayed and sang, then little rooms where they slept. There's the kitchen, and the kitchen garden. Then they had an area where they looked after sick people, and work places where they copied manuscripts or made herbal medicines. They had store houses. Look, there's a grain store.'

Iain's spine tingled. 'A grain store!' he thought. 'That's what Mum said the Granary was.' He raised his hand.

'Yes, Iain?' said Fattie, who was now walking round the classroom as they all looked at the illustration in the book.

'Did the – er – the Carthusian Monastery have a grain store?'

'Oh yes, it would have.'

'Was that where the Granary Restaurant is now?'

Fattie laughed. 'Well, that's what they say.'

'What's ber meal?' asked Iain.

'Ber meal, or bere, is an old name for barley.'

'And what does "no bees" mean?'

Fattie bent his long frame down and asked quietly, so that the others couldn't hear, 'Where did you hear that?'

'The man in the long robe – the monk – said it. He was counting his beads. Maybe he really said, "No beads", but that'd be silly, 'cause he had beads.'

'Beads?' said Fattie. 'What kind of beads?'

'*I* don't know,' Iain cried. 'He had a string of beads with a cross hanging from it, a wooden cross.'

'A rosary. Ah, now I understand. He was saying a prayer in Latin.'

'Why was he saying it in Latin?' asked Iain.

'It goes back to the time when everyone used Latin in the Church. It was an international language, understood all over Europe.'

'Is "No bees" Latin for something?'

'Yes,' said Fattie. 'There was a prayer that went, "*Ave Maria, gratia plena, dominus tecum. Ora pro nobis . . .* ". That's "Hail Mary, full of grace, God is with you. Pray for us . . . ". *Nobis* means "for us".'

Iain felt all this was getting a bit beyond him and sucked his pencil.

'Where did you hear this?' Fattie asked again.

'In the Granary. I saw an old monk.' Iain was getting tired of repeating the same thing.

The teacher looked at him seriously for a minute or two, then shook his head. He walked back to his desk and called for everyone's attention to go on with the lesson. Iain didn't really listen to him, because he was so full of his new discovery. He was already starting to wonder if he would have another glimpse into the past and what it might be. He had heard about people who could foresee the future but he'd never heard of anyone who could look back into the days of 'Once upon a time'. It was clear that neither his mother nor Mr McFatridge believed him, so it wasn't likely anyone else would. His pals were probably laughing at him and, as for his father, Iain hoped his mother wouldn't mention it to him or there would be an almighty row. He'd just have to keep it a secret between himself and Bitsy and wait and see what happened next.

2

Battle on the Inch

Gran and Grandpa Cameron lived on the other side of Perth, beside the North Inch, not far from the old Perth Bridge. Gran Cameron was tall and thin, with a long bony neck and purple cheeks. She made Iain think of the turkey they'd got at Christmas from Hay's Mart. Even when she spoke, she had a gobbly sort of voice. 'Chew your food, Iain,' she would say, every time they went for tea, only it came out as 'Choogle your foogle, Iain.'

Iain was always in a hurry to finish his tea so that he could go and find his grandpa in the back room. Grandpa Cameron always managed to be too busy to come and sit at the tea table. 'I've a few things to attend to,' he would say, pulling at his pipe.

'Did you mengle the fan heegle?' Gran would ask.

'Mend the fan heater?' Grandpa would echo. 'Just about to start on it.'

Before he retired, Grandpa Cameron had had an electric shop in the town and was, as Iain's mum told him every time they went to visit – which was every week – a Master Electrician. Iain always thought of the words as having capital letters because that was the way his mum said them. The back room was full of electric gadgets in different stages of repair, tools and instruments of all sorts, as well as wire, plugs, flex, switches, light bulbs and any number of bits and pieces that defied description.

Iain loved the back room, where he could spend hours poking around, connecting any odds and ends his grandpa let him play around with into wonderful imaginary inventions. But he knew the real reason why Grandpa worked there such a lot. In one corner, behind a screen, there was a table where Grandpa carefully cut and shaped pieces of fine wood, which he glued together, buffed and polished, fitted with strings, pegs and bridges. It took him a long time, because the work was done with such gentle precision and loving skill, bit by bit. On the wall above the table hung one specimen of the finished article – a fiddle! Grandpa was a secret fiddle maker, or so it seemed to Iain. Gran never ever referred to the fact that fiddles were made in her house and Iain never knew where the completed ones went. Sometimes Grandpa would take the fiddle down and play it.

'What would you like, Iain?' he would ask in his quiet Highland voice. 'A reel or a waltz?'

'A reel! A reel!' Iain would cry, because reels were fast and lively.

'You're a true Lochaber man,' Grandpa would say, and Iain often wondered what that meant. One day his grandpa told him about the Highland clans.

'A clan was just a family, a big family. The chief was the father of the family. The chief of my clan is Cameron of Locheil.'

'What did clans do?' Iain now wanted to know. His grandpa laughed as he hung the fiddle back on the wall. 'Mostly they fought each other.'

'Was that the War?' asked Iain. He'd heard his grandpa talk about the War, in which he had been a soldier.

'Oh no, no, laddie,' replied Grandpa. 'I'm talking about long, long ago.' He sat down to repair a toaster, so Iain wandered back to the sitting-room.

Outside, the Inch was bathed in evening sunlight. It was even better for playing football on than the South Inch, because it had a number of football pitches, with goal-posts, which were used by local teams. 'Can I go and play on the Inch, Mum?' he asked.

'Just for a wee while,' she agreed.

'Dongle get your feegle wet,' said Gran.

Iain didn't answer but he burned with indignation. Get his feet wet! Did she think he was going to paddle in the Tay? He opened the front door and ran down the steps and across the tree-lined road to the verge of the rolling expanse of green that lay along the riverside, with the gardens of the big houses in Bridgend opposite and the blue-grey peaks of the Grampians to the north.

It was a quiet evening with not many people about. Iain ran on to the grass and ran, and ran, and ran. He wished Bitsy were with him, but Bitsy always had to be left at home when they visited Gran and Grandpa. Iain ran round the Olympic circuit and won a gold medal, then competed in the Commonwealth Games where he scored a hat-trick, and finally threw himself down on the cool grass beneath one of the big trees. With his eyes shut, he breathed in the smell of the earth, which he quite liked.

'I wonder,' he thought to himself, 'if the earth smelled like this long ago?' He didn't know much about long ago, he had to admit. Any ideas he had were vague and shadowy.

He was almost drifting into a doze, 'dovering', as his dad would say, when he heard a far-off clashing noise and the faint sound of people cheering and yelling, which got heavier and heavier and louder and louder, till he seemed to be in the middle of it. He was frightened to death, but he opened his eyes and found himself looking at the back of a pair of very strong, very dirty bare legs. He jumped to his feet and discovered he was at the back of a crowd of men, all facing the other way, all wearing tattered and stained plaids, belted round their middles, all cheering loudly. He couldn't see past the men, so he jumped up and down, like a performing flea. It wasn't that they were really so very tall. They weren't as tall as his dad or his grandpa, but they were very sturdy-looking and had long hair and beards.

Suddenly their ranks parted, the men fell back on both sides, as a man bigger and stronger than any of them came striding forward. He was wearing a rough, belted tunic, open at the neck. It seemed to be him the folk were cheering. Iain listened to what they were shouting but it seemed to be in a different language. 'I wonder if it's Latin?' he thought, remembering the monk in the Granary. He didn't know who these men were, but they certainly were not monks! As he listened he could only pick out two words that seemed to be repeated over and over again by the cheering mob. One was 'glayva' and the other was 'hal'. Neither of them made sense to him.

The big man smiled and nodded and waved a great sword above his head and, as the light from the sinking sun glinted on the blade, Iain saw that it was bright red and dripping. He turned away, closing his eyes and feeling sick.

'Oh no!' he thought. 'It must be blood! He must have been killing someone! Maybe there was a battle.' Grandpa's words came back to him about the clans fighting each other long ago. 'Long ago!' It was his gift again, showing him something from the past.

He opened his eyes but the men had all vanished. The Inch was peaceful again and becoming shadowy in the dusk.

'Iain!' called mum from the door of the house. 'Time to come in. We're going home.'

As they walked through the town, Iain asked her, 'What does "Glayva" mean?'

'Where did you hear that?'

'Oh, I just heard a man on the Inch say it.' He knew better than to start trying to convince his mother that he'd seen a battle.

'Maybe he'd been to the George Hotel!' she laughed.

'Why?'

'It's the name of a liqueur; a drink. It comes from Gaelic.'

'What does it mean?'

'Very good!'

'Very good,' repeated Iain. 'Well, that makes sense at least.'

'They were obviously very pleased with the man with the sword,' he thought, 'maybe pleased because he'd killed whoever he'd killed.'

Next day at school Iain asked Fattie, 'Was there ever a battle on the North Inch?'

'Why yes,' he said. 'I thought everyone in Perth knew that. It's quite famous. In fact, if you take a look, there's a plaque with the name and date on, just at the beginning of Rose Terrace. Haven't you seen it?'

'No,' said Iain, 'but I must have walked past it dozens of times.'

'Have a look for it the next time you're there,' Fattie told him. 'What made you ask about it?'

Iain looked at him and shrugged his shoulders. 'If I tell you, you won't believe me. You didn't believe me when I told you about the monk in the Granary.'

'Try me,' said Fattie. So Iain told him about the cheering men with their plaids and swords and the big man with the blood on his sword and the cries of 'Hal' and 'Glayva'. He kept his voice down so that the rest of the class wouldn't hear. He expected Fattie to laugh at him, but this time he didn't. He stood for a moment staring at Iain, then said, 'Come and talk to me at lunchtime in the staff-room.'

Iain's friend, Neil 'Sobersides', overheard this and gave him a dark look. 'Are you in trouble with Fattie?' he asked.

'No,' said Iain.

'What does he want to talk to you about then?'

'I don't know,' said Iain. He didn't feel like telling Neil about what he had seen on the Inch. He'd think he had gone daft. Several of the class had overheard Fattie telling him to come to the staff-room and were curious to know why. When he told them he didn't know, they didn't believe him and one or two started calling him teacher's pet and a sook or made gestures to suggest he had a screw loose.

When he knocked at the staff-room door, Fattie appeared with a cup of coffee and a roll. 'Have you had your lunch, Iain?' he asked.

'Yes,' said Iain. It wasn't quite true. He'd hastily scoffed a packet of crisps, but he'd been much too excited to tackle the packed lunch his mother had given him.

'Follow me into the classroom while I eat mine.'

They went into the classroom and sat at Fattie's table. 'Now,' he said, when he had emptied his cup, 'tell me that story again.'

So Iain described the cheering and shouting men and the big man with the reddened sword blade. Fattie listened, then was silent for a few moments.

'You're quite sure,' he said at last, 'that you'd never heard of the battle on the Inch before?'

'Never,' Iain assured him.

'It was called the Battle of the Clans.'

'Which clans?' asked Iain. 'My Grandpa's clan is Cameron.'

'Well, according to the records, it was Clan Chattan and Clan Kay.'

'Never heard of them,' said Iain.

'Yet you saw them!'

'Do you think so?' Iain really wanted to hear Fattie say he believed him. His teacher looked at him long and hard.

'I've always found you truthful, Iain,' he said. 'But you have to admit, this takes a bit of swallowing.'

'I know,' said Iain.

'That big man. What did you say they were shouting at him?'

'Well,' said Iain, 'it sounded like "Glayva" and "Hal". My Mum says Glayva is a drink and it's Gaelic for "very good".'

'That's right. And Hal is the man's name.'

'How do you know?'

'That's the story,' said Fattie. 'Hal o the Wynd or Henry Wynd. He was a weaver and he took part in the battle because one side was short of a man. I can never remember which one it was:

Hal o the Wynd he taen the field
Alang by the skinklin Tay
An he hackit doun the men o Chattan
Or was it the men o Kay?

Whan aa was owre he dichted his blade
And steppit awa richt douce
To draik his drouth in the Skinners' Vennel
At clapperin Clemmy's hoose.

Hal o the Wynd had monie a bairn
And bairns' bairns galore
Wha wud speer aboot the bluidy battle
And what it was fochten for.

'Guid faith, my dawties, I never kent;
But yon was a dirlin day
When I hackit doun the men o Chattan
Or was it the men o Kay?'

'What's that?' asked Iain, chuckling in spite of himself.

'Oh, it is a poem by a man called Willie Soutar. He lived in Perth not so long ago. You'll see his house in Wilson Street.'

Iain said nothing. He wasn't too keen on poetry as a rule. Miss Proudfoot, the teacher he'd had before the one who shouted, had been mad keen on it and was always launching into sloppy verses about flowers and birds and springtime, which had put Iain right off for life, or so he thought. But he was quite tickled by these words and the way Fattie had spoken them. Also, they'd been about something he'd seen himself.

Just then, the bell rang for the end of lunchtime. Fattie got up. 'Right then, Iain. That was an interesting talk we've had. Let me know if you have any more visions of the past, will you?'

'You don't think I'm just making it up?'

Fattie looked at him quite seriously. 'Mmmmmm, we-e-ell,' he said, 'I don't think so.'

The rest of the class started to come in so there was no time to say any more. But at the end of the afternoon, as Iain was going out of the school entrance, Fattie drove past him slowly with his car window wound down and called, 'Remember, Iain. Anything you see, tell me.'

'I will,' Iain promised. Then, running alongside the car, he called, 'Mr McFatridge!'

The teacher stopped the car.

'Yes?'

'Why do you think I can see – well, things like I told you?'

Fattie shook his head with a bemused smile. 'I haven't a clue, laddie. I haven't a clue!' With a wave of his hand he was gone.

Iain went home none the wiser, but somehow comforted to know that Fattie shared his secret and didn't just think he was talking nonsense. He hugged Bitsy on the hearthrug after his dinner and whispered in his ear, 'Now it's you and me and Fattie!'

3

The Tinker Woman and the Magic Chanter

It seemed like a long time to Iain before he had any more visions. In the meantime, life went on as usual, with Mum and Dad and Bitsy and school and visits to Gran and Grandpa Cameron. He found the plaque Fattie had spoken about, near his gran's house. It was on a neat stone block and read: 'The Battle of the Clans 1396'.

It seemed very ordinary and uninteresting compared with the wild and extraordinary scene he had glimpsed. 'They should have had a statue of Hal o the Wynd and his big sword,' he thought to himself. It seemed rather weird that the only battles that took place on the Inch now were football matches.

Iain, who had always liked to kick a ball about, was delighted when the boys in his class and the one above it started to get football practice at school. Every Wednesday after school Mr Lornie the gym teacher showed them new turns, tackles and passes. With the fine spring weather and the lighter evenings, Iain went out with Bitsy after dinner to practice his football skills. He'd got a football as a Christmas present, and a pair of boots for his last birthday.

Playing, of course, for St Johnstone, he'd dribble the ball past imaginary opponents, pass to an unseen winger, then race forward to receive the return and go on to score goal after goal. All the time he would keep up a running commentary – in more senses than one – like the man on the television sports programmes.

'Barlass, the wonder boy, has the ball! He's challenged by Strachan. He beats Strachan. He's down the field like an electric hare. Miller tries to stop him. He dodges round Miller. Then he passes to Baker. Baker shoots. It hits the bar! It ricochets to Barlass. Barlass heads it back to Baker. Baker shoots. The ball looks spot on. The goalie comes out and deflects it. Barlass shoots. IT'S A GOAL!'

Occasionally Iain's goal shots went wide and landed in the bushes, whereupon Bitsy would go and retrieve the ball, pushing it out in front of him with his nose. One sunny evening on the Inch when Iain was playing for Scotland in the World Cup, one of his goal shots veered away behind a big rhododendron bush. Bitsy dived after it but when he reappeared, the object he was rolling in front of him was not Iain's football. It was a black drawstring bag which jingled as it rolled. As Iain picked it up, a head peered round the rhodie and a hoarse voice called out, 'Hey, you, dug! Bring that back!'

As Iain ran towards the bush, a sturdy figure in a buttoned-up checked tweed coat and a red headscarf stepped out. Iain recognised who it was right away. It was old Lizzie Blackie, a woman who came round the doors collecting rags and selling white heather and other odds and ends from a basket. At first Iain thought she was very angry but, as he drew near, he saw that she was frightened.

'It's all right!' he called. 'I've got it. Here's your bag.'

Old Lizzie grabbed it and peered inside anxiously, then she grinned at Iain, her weather-beaten face breaking up into a thousand wrinkles. 'Thank you, son,' she said in a gentle throaty voice.

'Bitsy thought it was my ball,' Iain explained. By this time Bitsy had found the ball and had rolled it to Iain's feet. 'Is your bag all right?'

'Aye, son,' she said. 'It's fine. You're a good boy.' She went back to the bench where she had left her basket and sat down to open the bag again. Iain dribbled the ball till he was near enough to see that she was counting money, mostly coins, and that she had quite a lot of them.

'That must be the money she gets for her rags and the other things she sells,' he thought. She caught sight of him watching her and closed the bag. He smiled at her and Bitsy went forward and sniffled at her old scuffed boots. She bent forward and patted the dog's head, keeping her bright, dark eyes on Iain.

'Come here a minute, son,' she said.

He went and sat beside her on the the park bench. 'Let me see your hand,' she asked. Mystified, Iain held out his hand and she turned it over and looked intently into his palm. What she saw seemed to surprise her. 'God bless me, baby!' she cried. 'Who gave you a hand like this?'

Iain was not too happy about being called 'baby' – he was, after all, nine years old but he was so keen to know what she found so special about his hand that he said nothing.

'This is a very lucky hand,' Lizzie went on, gazing solemnly into Iain's face with her wise old eyes. 'Very lucky indeed. Tell me, baby, do you ever see things that other people don't see?'

Iain was flabbergasted. How did she know his secret?

'It's in your hand,' she said. 'The lines can't lie.' He was dying to ask her more about it but she suddenly gathered up her basket and drawstring bag and began to stump off. Turning, she gave Iain another crinkly smile and said, 'I'll speak to you again, son. Look out for me. I've got to go now and make my man's tea.'

'All right,' said Iain.

'It was good o ye to save my bag.' She hurried away, while Iain looked after her thoughtfully. He *had* to talk to her again. He must catch her next time she passed that way. Bitsy barked to remind him that they had an important World Cup fixture to finish before it got too dark to play.

'Come on, Bitsy!' he shouted. 'Scotland's playing Brazil! Let's go!'

It was some time before he saw old Lizzie again and not before he'd had another of his visions. Iain always got up extra early on a Saturday morning, so as to make it as long a day as possible. His mum could never understand why she had to drag him out of bed for school, yet on Saturdays he was up before the milkman. It was strange, Iain thought, how dim some parents were. The first thing he did was to sit on the window-sill with Bitsy to see what he could see on the Inch, which usually wasn't very much.

One particular morning early in June, when it was light very, very early and there was a white, moving mist on the grass, Iain looked out of his window and saw, not the familiar expanse of grass circled by trees, bushes and flowerbeds, but a rather rougher-looking green on which a group of men were standing with bows and arrows. At first he wondered if this was some new sports club come for early morning practice. After all, he and his dad had watched the archery competitions in the Olympic Games on television the year before. But these men looked very different from the Olympic marksmen, and their bows and arrows were nothing like the ones on television. They wore belted plaids over buff-coloured shirts, had beards and shoulder-length hair and stood in a semi-circle, laughing and shouting to one another. Then each one in turn took aim at a target that stood in front of a mound. Iain saw that all the arrows hit it fair and square – these were very good bowmen.

Iain watched fascinated as one by one they drew back their bowstrings and the arrows smacked repeatedly into the middle of the circle. Just then a man on a small shaggy pony came galloping towards the butts, shouting and waving. He was wearing a blue glengarry bonnet. Whatever the news he brought was, all the bowmen cheered and leapt about in excitement. Iain had just pulled up the window to see if he could hear more clearly, when Mum's voice rang out behind him. 'Iain! Breakfast's ready!' She was at the door of his room. 'Goodness, you'll have to tidy this room today!'

'Oh, Mum!' he pleaded, 'I've got football practice this morning, and this afternoon Neil and I were going to the shows. We've saved up for it.'

'That's okay,' said his mother, 'as long as, somewhere in between, you tidy your room. You can do it after breakfast.'

'All right, Mum,' said Iain with a sigh. He turned to look out of the window again but all he saw was the top of an Edinburgh-bound bus and the familiar trees lining the Inch. There was no sign of the archers or the horseman; just a man walking his dog and two boys with fishing-rods making towards the river.

After breakfast, Iain pushed everything lying on the floor of his room under the bed, threw his library books and his spaceman robot into the wardrobe and scooped up all the bits of Lego, jigsaw pieces, marbles, model cars and unrecognisable plastic thingmybobs into a plastic bag.

'There!' he said. 'Mum can't complain about that!'

He took his football kit and went downstairs. Neil was waiting for him on the Inch and together with Bitsy they staged an imaginary cup final between Rangers and St Johnstone.

'Are you coming to the shows today?' asked Neil at last when they were all out of breath.

'Of course,' said Iain. 'I've got four pounds fifty saved up. How much have you got?'

'Four pounds sixty-five,' replied Neil. 'Let's put it all together and half it.'

'Okay. Meet you at two o'clock at the corner.'

At the corner, where the gate into the showground was, Iain spied his friend waiting and ran towards him. About twice a year the dark-eyed show people came with their beautiful trailers and trucks to set up the gaudily lit roundabouts and rides, sideshows and stalls. The bare park was turned into a wonderland of whirling colours and deafening music. People flocked in from Perth and all the country villages roundabout and the loud noise which blared out across the Inch could even be heard across the

River Tay. Iain really looked forward to the shows and had saved up his pocket money for weeks just for today.

Now he and Neil ran from the Silver Speedway to the Moonrocket, then into the Ghost Train; the ground beneath their feet throbbing with the noise and bustle all around them. The names of the rides were picked out in coloured lights that flashed on and off, and raucous voices rang out from all the sideshows. 'Aa the lucky numbers! Hit the target and win the jackpot! Five shots for ten pence!'

Iain loved the exhilaration of whizzing round and round on the Silver Speedway, but his favourite sideshow was the Rifle Range. Here he spent the last of his money and at the third attempt won a goldfish in a water-filled plastic bag. Neil had won a toy panda at the Hoopla Stall. They had each gorged themselves on a huge pink cloud of candy floss and were well pleased with their afternoon.

As they were working their way back through the jostling crowds and the hubbub of music to the way out, Iain began to hear another sound that rose above all the rest. 'Someone's playing the pipes!' he yelled into Neil's ear. They soon found who it was. Near the entrance to the showground, a magnificent figure was striding up and down. He was so tall, he seemed like a giant, and so broad that he looked twice the size of anyone else around. He wasn't toshed up in a kilt and plaid and feather bonnet, the way pipers usually are, but was just wearing an old jacket and baggy trousers with a cloth cap on his head. His face was brown and strong-looking, and his leathery fingers wagged up and down fast and furious on the pipe chanter. The tune he was playing made Iain want to march and swagger too.

'Who on earth is that?' Neil shouted.

Iain shook his head and shrugged his shoulders. They just stood and listened to the piper until he stopped. Then he tucked the pipes under his arm and turned to someone standing behind him. To his surprise, Iain recognised old Lizzie Blackie with her basket. He moved nearer and heard the piper say, 'Well, wee woman, will ye feck me a puckle lour?'

Iain had no idea what that meant. 'Perhaps he's talking Gaelic,' he thought.

Lizzie rummaged in her basket and pulled out the drawstring bag and gave the piper some money from it. He took it with a smile and was walking away when she laughingly called after him, 'Dinna come back peevie!' He waved without turning round and continued on his way out of the showground and across the street. Lizzie recognised Iain and gave him her warm smile. Her basket was full of the most beautiful red and yellow blooms.

'Hallo, son,' she said. 'Have ye had a good time at the shows?'

'Yes, thanks,' said Iain. 'Look, I won a fish!'

'That's lovely!'

'What are these?' asked Iain, pointing to her flowers for they seemed like something from a tropical forest.

'They're widden flooers, son. I mak them masel, oot o the bourtree.'

'Do you know that piper?'

Lizzie laughed. 'I should, son. That's my man, Geordie.'

'Geordie? I thought you called him Peevie just now.'

Lizzie doubled up with laughter, covering her face with her hand. At last she managed to gasp, 'He's awa tae the pub. Geordie's his name.'

'Then what was Peevie?'

'I'll tell ye anither time, son.'

'I wish *I* could play the pipes like that,' said Iain with a sigh.

'Dae ye, son? Dae ye, baby?' Old Lizzie's dark eyes glowed at him.

'I'd like it fine,' he said, and he knew he really meant it.

'Why's that, son?' asked Lizzie, still looking intently into his face.

'I don't know really,' he replied truthfully. 'But when I hear them I feel kind of . . . alive all over.'

Lizzie laid a calloused hand on his shoulder. 'It's in your bluid, baby.'

'Sounds as if you've got a fever,' said Neil. Iain had clean forgotten he was with him. Neil added in a whisper, 'Who's this dirty old bag?'

Iain turned to him and whispered in fierce embarrassment, 'This is old Lizzie Blackie and she's not dirty. She's . . . she's . . . ' He couldn't find the word he was looking for, but he knew it meant something like an old stone or an old tree weathered by the wind and sun.

Lizzie seemed not to have heard Neil's rude remark. 'Watch for me on the Inch, son,' she told him. 'I'll be there in a day or two and I'll have something for ye.'

'Right,' said Iain.

'What's your name, son?'

'Iain.'

'Iain! That's a richt guid name, Iain. That wis ma father's name.' She settled her basket on her arm. 'Well, I'll need to go an find Geordie. I'll see ye, when I see ye.' She stumped off in the same direction that Geordie had taken and as Iain and Neil watched she turned into the door of a small pub.

'What does she mean,' asked Neil, 'she'll "have something for you"?'

'How should I know?' retorted Iain. Whatever it was, it was exciting to think about, but for Neil's benefit he pretended to scoff. 'She was just blethering.'

For the next few days he kept his eyes skinned when he was on the Inch, looking for old Lizzie, but in the meantime he told Fattie about the archers he had seen.

'That's just where the old bow butts were,' his teacher told him. 'That's where they would practice. But what about this horseman who came? What was he wearing?'

'A plaid, of course, and a blue bonnet. It wasn't really a horse he was on, just a kind of rough pony.'

'It'd be what they called "a garron",' said Fattie. 'Wearing a blue bonnet? Could he have been a Jacobite, I wonder? Maybe a bit early for that. What news was he bringing? Perhaps he'd come to tell them the Prince had landed and was coming to Perth with the Athole men. Or maybe they were Wallace's men hearing the news from Stirling Bridge.'

'What's all that about?' asked Iain in bewilderment.

'Haven't you heard of William Wallace or Bonnie Prince Charlie?'

'Well, yes, but I don't know much about them.'

'We'll come to that in history, don't worry,' said Fattie. History had almost become Iain's favourite subject, next to football.

Five days after meeting old Lizzie at the shows, Iain saw her on the Inch, near the rhododendron bush where Bitsy had run off with her bag. She beckoned to him and when he ran over to her, she took something out of her basket and held it out to him. It was a long pipe of black wood, fat at one end and thin at the other, with holes along it and a mouthpiece.

'What is it?' asked Iain.

'It's a practice chanter,' said Lizzie, 'for learning the pipes. It was Geordie's grandfather's grandfather's. Geordie's put a new reed in it for you.'

'Oh!' gasped Iain, 'thank you, but . . . '

She leaned forward and said to him very quietly and deliberately, as if the words were very, very important, 'It's a magic chanter.'

'What does it do?'

'It'll keep you awake when you go up the Sleepy Glen.'

'What do you mean?'

'You'll find out, baby, you'll find out.'

She smiled at him mysteriously but with such warmth that he

suddenly saw what a beautiful old woman she was. On that sunny day, she was not wearing her usual headscarf and her black shiny hair was plaited into a loose bun at the nape of her neck. She wore dangling gold ear-rings and round her neck were strings of pearl beads.

Before Iain could ask her any more questions, she turned and hurried away. He fingered the chanter, then tried to blow through it, but couldn't make a sound. He sat down on the grass and experimented with it, trying to cover the holes with his fingers as he had seen Geordie do. He blew again but it was like one of those balloons that you get in every packet that just won't inflate and make your face turn purple.

'Magic chanter, indeed!' he thought indignantly. 'I never realised playing the pipes was so hard.' He kept trying and at last produced an awful bleating noise like a demented sheep. Bitsy started to howl in protest so he stopped.

'I don't think I'll let Mum see this,' he decided, so when he went home he slipped upstairs to his room and hid it, before going for his tea.

'I wonder what old Lizzie meant when she talked about the Sleepy Glen,' he thought as he lay in bed that night. 'She said I'd find out, and I mean to do just that.'

4

The Sleepy Glen

It was June and Iain began to dream about the greatest event of the term as far as he was concerned – the hill-walk in Glenisla. The very thought of being far away from the town, among hills alive with pheasants, foxes and hares, could only be described as double-doss – the word he and Neil used for anything out of this world.

'Saturday, twenty-first of June,' Mum read from the letter he brought home from school, 'by bus to Ardbeth beyond Alyth, walk five miles from there to Inchbeg. Cost of trip five pounds, to include bus and packed lunch.'

'Not bad,' said Dad. 'Do you think you can walk all that way?'

'Of course I can!' said Iain.

'How do you get back from Inchbeg?'

'The bus goes on ahead and waits for us.'

'You'd better wear your tracksuit,' said Mum. 'The air's always cooler up in the hills.'

'Make sure you wear strong shoes,' added Dad. 'Trainers are useless for rough ground. There's nothing worse than trying to walk with sore feet or burst shoes.'

Iain was hardly listening – he was too busy thinking about the winding hill paths and the tumbling silver burns and the springy heather cowes you could lie on and look up to the sky where the larks and the peesies cried.

When the great morning arrived, Iain and Neil turned up at Tay Street, where the bus was waiting to leave at eight o'clock. Fattie, Mr Lornie and another teacher, Miss Paton, helped everyone to get seated. 'We'll be back at seven o'clock tonight,' Mr Lornie told the parents. 'We'll stop on the way for chips, probably at Blairgowrie.'

With a lot of cheering and waving, they were on their way, over the Queen's Bridge and past Bridgend to Isla Road, which would take them along past Old Scone and out into open country. Fattie stood at the front of the bus and issued a few warnings. 'Don't wander off on your own. Don't drop litter. Try to keep to firm ground. If there's a path, stay on it.'

Soon they were singing, clapping hands and stamping feet. They'd just got to the end of a mammoth version of 'Old Macdonald had a Farm', that incorporated some very unlikely livestock such as gorillas and elephants, when Miss Paton called out, 'That's enough now, boys and girls. Settle down, we're nearly there.'

Along the switchback road from Blairgowrie to Alyth they sped, past the green to the other side of the village, where they began to ascend more slowly towards the glen. They were to stop a bit along the road, at a place where they could take a path into the hills and follow it to where the bus would pick them up again. It wasn't a very long walk, but then some of the children had never been on a hill-walk before, so it was wise not to try to do too much. 'If you enjoy it,' Mr Lornie had said, 'you can try to walk further next time.'

'This should be it,' said Fattie, peering out of the front window of the bus. The driver pulled up gently and they all filed out. The boot was opened up and everyone got a lunch pack to put in their rucksack. 'We'll stop about twelve o'clock,' said Fattie. 'Driver, we'll meet you at four o'clock at Inchbeg.'

The bus moved away along the glen road and disappeared round the next corner, while the three teachers unfolded the map to check their position. Mr Lornie looked at the map several times, then scanned the surrounding area, a puzzled expression on his lean, tanned face. 'That's funny,' he said at last.

'Is there something wrong, Charlie?' asked Fattie. Mr Lornie drew him aside and laid the map on a flat stone. The two men pored over it for a few minutes, pointing to things on it, then pointing up and down the glen. Miss Paton fussed impatiently over the pupils, while Iain champed at the bit, raring to get going on that hill path. Eventually, Fattie came back to the group.

'Sorry to keep you waiting, but this map doesn't seem to be quite correct. There's a glen here that isn't on it!' The children stared, hardly understanding what he was saying. 'Never mind. The signpost says, "Inchbeg, five miles", so we'll just take this road.'

'I'll lead off,' said Mr Lornie. 'Now, just follow at your own pace. Don't try to keep up with people moving faster than you can. But don't lag too far behind.'

'I'll stay at the back to help the stragglers,' said Fattie.

'Girls,' said Miss Paton, 'remember to look for interesting plants and flowers.' The girls giggled. Plants and flowers were the last things on their minds.

'Can we buy Coke anywhere?' asked one. Miss Paton ignored the question.

The group set out up the fairly steep path and soon they were strung out in twos and threes behind Mr Lornie. Iain and Neil were near the front of the procession as it wound through clumps of golden broom, silvery birch trees, wild willow and bracken. Many large round stones reared up among the greenery and here and there were bits of crumbled masonry, where once perhaps there had been a croft. Nobody remarked on these ruins, not even when they saw, down by the swift-flowing burn, the remnants of an old mill wheel.

It was a warm sunny day with a haze that made the hillsides shimmer and waver almost like water. Birdsong echoed all around them and Fattie would look through his binoculars and call out from the rear, 'There's a pheasant,' or 'Look, a moorhen!'

'You don't need binoculars to see them,' Neil whispered to

Iain. 'We're practically tripping over them!' Iain's laughter was interrupted by a rumble from his tummy and he thought longingly of the lunch he was carrying.

At long last, Miss Paton shouted, 'Lunch!' and they all sat down on hummocks and ledges, tore open their lunch packs and downed the contents as if they had been starved for a week. Sausage rolls, egg sandwiches, buttered scones and chocolate biscuits all disappeared at ragtime speed, washed down with cartons of milk or orange juice.

Iain had brought the magic chanter with him, even though he couldn't play it. He moved into a little hollow behind a clump of broom, took it out and fingered it. Then he put the chanter to his lips and blew half-heartedly. To his amazement, a lovely true note came out of it. He tried covering some of the holes and blew again. Another fine note greeted him. He lifted and lowered his fingers and got more notes. Then somehow, he found himself playing a tune.

'This is strange,' he thought, 'it must be magic, right enough. I don't really know what I'm doing – my fingers seem to be moving by themselves! This is a great tune I'm playing!' After playing the tune through a few times, he decided to find Neil and show off his new-found skill, but when he ran up from the hollow and round the broom bushes, he couldn't believe his eyes. There were all his classmates, Mr Lornie, Fattie and Miss Paton all lying fast asleep!

Then he remembered old Lizzie's words when she gave him the chanter. 'This'll keep ye awake when ye go up the Sleepy Glen.' She must have been talking about this mysterious little glen that wasn't on the map – this must be the Sleepy Glen! Lizzie must be gifted with special knowledge of things like this. 'I wonder if the magic chanter can waken everyone up,' he thought. He put it to his lips again and it played the same lively tune, but not one of the sleeping folk stirred a hand or a foot, or a finger or a toe, or even a lash of an eye.

Iain became aware of another sound, so he stopped playing and recognised with a shiver of delight the sound of bagpipes coming towards him down the hillside. If his tune had been a good one, this was ten times better – wild and full of grace notes, but with a lilting rhythm that was irresistible. Iain waited with bated breath to see who this master piper might be.

Round the corner came an extraordinary figure, a giant of a man who reminded him of Lizzie's man, Geordie, only this figure had a mane of black hair and beard. He had the bearing of a prince, but his plaid was tattered and he was barefoot, marching along with the ribbons on the drones of his pipes flying in the breeze.

Seeing Iain, he stopped and hailed him. 'Hallo there, Iain! It is yourself, then?'

Iain was confused. 'How do you know my name?' he asked.

'Oh, I know your name all right. Iain it is. Aren't you the lad with the magic chanter?'

'Well, yes, I suppose I am. I mean, it certainly seems to be magic. Who are you?'

'My name is Seamas Dhu,' said the big man proudly. His way of speaking reminded Iain of Grandpa Cameron.

'Where do you come from?'

'I come from here,' said Seamas Dhu. 'This is my home, this glen, *Gleann a' Chadail*, the Sleepy Glen, although once it was called *Gleann nam Beatha*, the Glen of Life.'

'I didn't think anyone lived here,' said Iain. 'We didn't see any houses on the way up.'

'Not in your time,' replied Seamas Dhu. 'But now you are in my time. Come with me.'

He turned and began to walk up the glen, back the way he had come. Iain followed him, burning with curiosity, and there before him was a wonderful scene. The hillsides were dotted with heather-thatched cottages, smoke curling up from their roofs. People and animals were everywhere; long-haired, dark-clad women were feeding hens and carrying creels, washing clothes in

the burn and spreading them to dry on the bushes; men in buff shirts, some with plaids, were sitting by their cottages smoking pipes, or plaiting straw ropes, or riding about on sturdy ponies; barefoot children were running about, some with sticks to keep the cattle from straying, others with baskets to pick berries or gather herbs; older children carried fish or rabbits for the pot, or a bag of meal from the mill. Everyone was busy. There was a mill with a water-wheel, a little kirk with a kirkyard up on the hillside and, in the distance among some trees, a roof with turrets that seemed to belong to a bigger sort of place.

Iain followed Seamas Dhu past all this and heard him being greeted on every side.

'A fine day, Hamish.'

'Will you mend my big pot for me, Hamish? I need it for the brose.'

'Who's the *gille beag ruadh* you have with you?'

'Why do they call you Hamish?' inquired Iain. 'You said your name was Seamas Dhu.'

'So it is. But in Gaelic when you speak to me, you say Hamish.'

'But they're not speaking Gaelic,' said Iain. 'I can understand them and I don't know Gaelic.'

'They are speaking Gaelic,' Seamas assured him. 'I've given you the power to understand it, otherwise your visit would be a waste of time.'

'I see,' said Iain, although he didn't really. 'Is that me they were asking about?'

'*Gille beag ruadh.* Little red-haired boy,' said Seamas, 'and so you are.'

'Where are we going?' Iain panted as they climbed a rocky path.

'To my camp,' said Seamas.

'Do you mend pots, then?' Iain found the breath to ask.

'Indeed I do, and I can make them too.'

'Is that your trade?'

'Oh, I have many trades. I make horn spoons and willow

baskets and I can even make you a dirk or a silver brooch.'

'You play the pipes as well?'

'Of course. I come from a family of pipers. I pipe to the laird.'

'Are we near your house yet?' Iain was beginning to feel that his legs were turning to jelly as Seamas continued to climb, something he did with the ease of a wild creature.

At last he said, 'Here we are!'

They reached a sheltered corrie from which they looked down on the crofts and pastures of the glen. There, among the heather and gorse, were two tents, unlike any tents Iain had seen before. They were rounded in shape and covered with what looked like rough blankets, secured to the ground with big stones. In front of one, a fire was lit and a rosy-faced woman sat on the ground beside it, with a baby on her lap. Two bigger girls sat on either side of her, one stirring a pot on the fire, the other holding a jug of milk. Out of the other tent poked the tanned face of a boy of about Iain's age with a mop of black hair.

'This is my family,' said Seamas. 'My wife is called Mairi Mor.'

'Who is this?' asked Mairi.

'My name's Iain.'

'This is the boy who has the chanter,' said Seamas.

Mairi held out a hand in welcome and smiled warmly. 'We'll call you Iain Ruadh,' she said. 'This is little Domnall, and this is Eilidh,' she pointed to the girl stirring the pot. 'And this is Bella.' The girl holding the milk smiled shyly without looking at Iain.

'I'm Seamas Beag,' said the dark-haired boy as he came out of the tent and stood by his father.

'Do you live in these tents all the time?' asked Iain. He had never thought of tents as dwelling places, but just for camping holidays. 'It must be great fun.'

'Well, I don't know about that,' said Seamas with a strange kind of laugh, 'but, yes, we do live in them. Our people have lived in tents for hundreds of years. We move about, you see, to carry on all our trades, and we can take them with us.'

'How do you make them?'

'I'll show you that another time,' said Seamas. 'We use hazel sticks, because they bend easily, and we fix them in the ground and put covers over them – any strong material we can get.'

'Are they warm?' Iain asked.

'Oh yes, indeed. They're always warm inside. See for yourself.'

Iain crawled inside one of the tents, which, on that hot June day, was like an oven, and rather smelly, like sweaty socks. He came out again quite quickly.

'Sit down now,' said Mairi Mor, 'and Eilidh will give you some brochans.'

'What's that?' asked Iain. He was handed a tin bowl full of stuff that looked a bit like porridge, which he didn't much fancy, but he tasted it with the horn spoon and found it had a delicious nutty taste. It was not in the least like the stuff Gran sometimes made, which was more like wallpaper paste.

As they sat round the fire after their meal, Seamas took out a chanter, just like Iain's, and began to play it. He stood on the lip of the corrie and sent the wild notes skirling into the blue air. Iain went and stood beside him and looked down on the glen. He was struck again that it was such a lived-in place. Everywhere he looked there were little crofts and patches of crops, a cow or two here and there, some pigs, a few hens, a goat or a shaggy pony, a lochan with ducks and swans, small carts laden with peat or heather and people; people on every hillside.

'Is this what the glen was like in your time?' Iain asked Seamas Dhu.

'Oh yes,' Seamas said, 'this is our home. Now where is your chanter, *mo ghille*? Let us have a tune together.'

Iain took out his chanter and together they played, first a march and then a reel, again the music coming out of Iain's fingers without his knowing what he was doing. Eilidh, Bella and Seamas Beag got up and danced while Mairi Mor clapped her hands and hooched with delight.

When they stopped, Iain looked up at Seamas and said earnestly, 'That was great! But I want to play the way you play. I mean, not the magic way, but *really* play.'

'You will, Iain.' Seamas told him, 'That will happen. Just wait and see. But not here.'

Iain looked again down the glen. 'What happened to all these people? Why are there no people here in my time?'

Seamas sighed. 'It's a long sad story, Iain; a long sad story.'

'Tell me,' said Iain. So they all sat round the fire, looking down the hillside through the peat reek, and Seamas began to tell the story of *Gleann a' Chadail*, the Sleepy Glen.

'Long ago, in my time, and before it, the glen was as you have seen it, full of people and crops and cattle. They were small crops, perhaps, and the cattle were not like the ones in your time, but the people were able to live and were happy together. They were poor, but they were used to being poor, and though they had many a hard time, they didn't think themselves any the worse for it. Oh, you should have known some of those folk! They were proud of their name, which was Mac an Dhu, and of course I was of them too. My family were the metal-workers of the clan, armourers, silversmiths and tinsmiths.'

'What sort of things did you make?' asked Iain.

'Swords and dirks; brooches and rings; pins for plaids; cooking pots and basins and jugs.' Seamas opened the pouch that hung from his belt and took out a collection of things which he laid on the ground. There was a circular brooch, two or three silver pins of different sizes, a horn spoon with a carved handle and a single large, round pearl.

'These are some of my own things,' Seamas said. 'This is my dirk, which I use to cut up food or to defend myself with, if anyone attacks me. This is a brooch to fasten my plaid. The pins are for that too. I use the spoon to eat my brochans.'

'You made them?' Iain was full of admiration, for the workmanship was fine.

'Oh yes,' replied Seamas. 'That's my trade. Here's one for you,' and he gave Iain one of the pins.

'Thanks!' said Iain. 'What's the spoon made of?'

'Deer-horn.'

'Did you have to shoot the deer?'

'No, no,' laughed Seamas. 'I leave that to the laird. But he gives me some of the horn after he's been hunting. Sometimes a stag dies and you find it lying, so you take the horn.'

'How do you make things from it?' wondered Iain, thinking of the huge antlers.

'Ah, that's my secret. I also make baskets of wild willow. See, Mairi has one beside her.' Mairi's basket was round and very neatly made with a plaited rim and a handle.

'I suppose everyone needs all these things,' said Iain, 'so you'll make a good living?'

'I did,' said Seamas, and his face clouded over. 'I did once.'

'What about this pearl? Where on earth do you get pearls away up here? I thought they came from the sea.'

'You get freshwater pearls from mussels in the burns and rivers. My father got that one in that wee lochan down there.' Seamas pointed to a stretch of water glinting down below them.

'You find them with a glass-bottomed jug to look through and a forked stick to lift them out. The laird gave me a bit of glass for my jug. It takes patience to find them, but there's plenty there. Now, look down the glen and I will show you the people who lived there and what happened to them. Look through the wood smoke and you will see what happened.'

Iain peered into the blue veil of reek from the fire and saw the outlines of the hills and hollows, the cottages and crofts, flicker and waver like images on an old film.

'There is the house of Eoghan Mac an Dhu, a man with great knowledge of medicines made from plants. He could cure any disease of man or beast.'

Somehow the smoke magnified the view of the house and,

standing before it, a tall grey-haired man with twinkling blue eyes.

'He could tell stories at a ceilidh that would keep everyone listening all night long, from sunset to sunrise.'

'Goodness!' exclaimed Iain, 'How boring!'

'Boring?' laughed Seamas Dhu. 'Why should it be boring?'

'Och,' said Iain, 'a story that goes on all night? Surely people would get fed up listening?'

'Not at all,' said Seamas Dhu. 'It's well seen that you've never heard a proper story in your life or you wouldn't say such a thing!'

'Oh, I've heard good stories,' Iain admitted, 'and I like good stories. But I could never listen to one that went on all night.'

Seamas Dhu snorted gently. 'Oh well, we'll see about that.'

'Is he the only one who tells stories?'

'Well, he's looked on as the best storyteller in the glen but, of course, everyone else can tell a story too. You see, when people get together in someone's house for a ceilidh – that's a visit – everyone has to take their turn.'

Iain groaned. 'That must be awful!'

Seamas Dhu looked at him and shook his head. 'My, aren't you the *amadan mor*! Do people in your time not know how to enjoy themselves?'

Iain didn't want to be rude, but to him the idea of everyone *having* to tell a story didn't appeal very much. 'But what if you don't know any stories?'

'Well, then, you can sing a song, play the pipes or the fiddle, dance, anything so long as you entertain your friends.'

'I don't think my friends would thank me for singing!' giggled Iain. 'Anyway, what if you can't do any of these things?'

Seamas smiled. 'In my time, everyone could do something, or were willing to try at least. That's the way we made our own entertainment. In your time it may be different.'

'It certainly is,' said Iain. 'You see, we have television and films and videos and cassettes. You can sit and watch and listen all day if you like. There's always something new.'

'Now that would be boring!' said Seamas. Iain stared at him in surprise and they both laughed.

'Come,' said Seamas. 'let's go to a ceilidh.'

The pictures through the wood smoke changed and Iain found himself looking into a room full of people, with logs blazing on a stone jutting out from the wall. There was a hole in the roof to take the smoke away but a lot of it lingered in the rafters.

People of all ages were sitting everywhere, on low stools, on the floor or on a long wooden settle with a high back. Most of the women were knitting or spinning. Someone was singing a song and every now and then everyone joined in a chorus of 'Ho ro hi'.

'This is the ceilidh house,' said Seamas. 'It belongs to Aonghais Mac an Dhu – that's the man singing by the fire. He's called the *fear an tigh*, the man of the house.'

'What is he singing? I can't follow it,' said Iain.

'It's a song about the great deeds of an ancestor of his, with the same name, Aonghais Mac an Dhu. He was as tall as a tree and had the strength of six men.'

'Sounds like boasting to me,' said Iain rather scornfully.

'Of course it is,' said Seamas. 'That's how you show you're proud of your ancestors.'

'What did his ancestor do?'

'Many things,' said Seamas. 'He slew Black Donald of the Skulls and he drove out the cattle thieves from Athole. They said he could lift with one hand a pine tree that had been felled, and he could leap across the White Linn from Hunter's Rock to the Lover's Crag.'

'Where are they?'

'Look over yonder,' Seamas told him, pointing to a huge boulder that almost crowned the opposite hillside. Water hung in a bridal veil of white froth between it and a smaller outcrop of rock.

Looking through the wood smoke into the ceilidh house, Iain saw that a piper was playing and almost the whole lot of them were now dancing in that confined space – old and young, men, women and children; all setting, turning and laughing at the fun. Iain recognised the tune as one of the reels Grandpa played on his fiddle. 'That must be an old tune,' he thought.

Then Eoghan Mac an Dhu began to tell a story, and Iain had never heard a story like it. Soon he forgot everything else and was aware only of the voice of the storyteller as he told a tale of high adventure, magicians and enchantments, stolen princesses, perilous journeys and impossible tasks, transformations, wild chases, life and death combats, incredible courage and evil trickery of all kinds. Iain moved in a world of dark castles, high hills, wide forests and magic lochs. It was as if the story was happening to him, and it was he who was on the quest for the long-lost princess, facing dragons, giants and witches, wielding an enchanted sword and wearing the cloak of darkness or the shoes of swiftness.

Suddenly, he found himself sitting with Seamas Dhu by the dying fire. Seamas was laughing at him. 'So this is Iain Ruadh who would be bored listening to a story all night?'

'All night!' echoed Iain.

'Well it's morning now!' said Seamas. 'See, the dawn's starting to brighten the sky.'

'I thought I'd been asleep and dreaming,' said Iain.

'Maybe you were, maybe you were,' said Seamas. 'What did you think of the ceilidh then?'

'Well, it was great! Everyone was together and they all knew one another, and they seemed to be having a lot of fun.'

'Of course,' said Seamas. 'So you see how sad it was for all that to come to an end?'

'Why did that happen?' asked Iain.

Seamas put more wood on the fire, making it blaze up, to keep them from the morning chill, and pointed to the house with the turrets among the trees. 'That is the castle of the chief of the Mac an Dhus, Domnall Ruraidh Mac an Dhu. Watch and you will see how that house became a curse on the people of the glen and how in turn it was destroyed by a curse.'

5

The Clearance

In the grey light of morning, Iain looked through the smoke from the fire and saw another story unfold before his eyes. He saw people coming from every part of the glen to stand in a great crowd round a green knowe near the wood where the castle was. He noticed the men were not wearing plaids, but roughly cut trousers or knee breeches and jackets. Then, from the trees, there emerged a group of four well-dressed and grand-looking people. There was a grey-haired man and a small grey-haired woman, a slim, handsome young man, dressed in satin and lace, and a pretty young woman wearing a silk dress with a velvet wrap.

'That is old Domnall Ruraidh; his wife, Dolina; their son, young Domnall Ruraidh; and his wife, Arabella. She is English. In fact, young Domnall Ruraidh went to school in England and is quite English spoken himself. He is certainly a stranger here. I think he means well, but his ways are not the ways of the people of the glen and he doesn't understand them any more than they understand him.'

'Why aren't they wearing tartan?' asked Iain.

'Oh, it has been forbidden to do so.'

'Who by? Not by Domnall Ruraidh surely?'

'No, no. By the King. By King George in London.'

Iain couldn't understand this at all. He watched as the old chief and his son walked up to the top of the green knowe and spoke to all those assembled at the bottom of the slope.

Iain noticed that around his neck he wore a thong with a piece of horn attached to it.

'My children,' he said, 'I have always loved you and cared for you. Now I am getting too old to be your chieftain. Today, my son is twenty-one years old, so I am handing over my estate to him. He has had the education of a fine gentleman and is very fit to manage things in this modern world. Please, for my sake, welcome him as your new laird.'

Everybody cheered and young Domnall Ruraidh bowed and smiled winningly to the crowd. 'I'm very pleased to meet you all,' he said, speaking in English rather than Gaelic, which meant many of them wouldn't understand him. 'I'm very much a stranger here, but I hope to get to know you better. I promise to do all I can to keep this glen a prosperous and well-run community. Now, you'll all come up to the castle tonight for a ceilidh.'

There was some polite applause, then an awkward pause during which people could be heard muttering, 'What did he say? I can't follow the English. Has he not the Gaelic?' Old Domnall Ruraidh intervened tactfully in Gaelic to tell them what his son had said. When they heard there was to be a ceilidh at the castle, of course, they cheered. From somewhere, a piper appeared and began to play and everyone danced, including the laird's family.

'Well, they all seem quite pleased,' said Iain. 'How did the house become a curse?'

Seamas kicked the wood in the fire, causing a shower of sparks to rise. 'Through greed and treachery,' he replied grimly. 'In spite of all his fair words, look what young Domnall Ruraidh did.'

Iain looked again through the smoky veil and saw another scene. He saw Eoghan Mac an Dhu come riding up the glen on a sturdy pony, with a leather satchel slung over his shoulder. At every road and track end leading up to crofts on the hillside, he stopped to speak to the men who were standing there. His face was very sad and he kept taking a paper out of his satchel and reading it to each person he met. It was obviously bad news, for some of them put their heads in their hands, others shook their fists and cursed, while others sat down on the ground and wept.

'What's happening?' asked Iain. 'What's he telling them?'

Seamas answered with his teeth clenched in rage. 'Eoghan has been to Edinburgh to see the new laird and discuss the rents of the crofts. They used to do that face to face with his father, on their own doorsteps. Now they have to go to an office in the city, where they don't even see the young laird, just his factor. Eoghan is telling them that they have to pay a very high new rent, a rent none of them can possibly afford, so they will all have to leave their homes and their little bits of land.'

'But I thought the land belonged to them,' said Iain.

'So it did. In the time of old Domnall Ruraidh and all those before him, they were clan chiefs and the land belonged to the clan. But now things have changed. There are no chiefs now, only landowners. Young Domnall, or Donald, Ruraidh is one of these new lairds – oh yes! There are plenty more like him. He wants the people off his land so that he can raise sheep. That's the coming thing. That's why he's fixing the rents so they can't pay. They'll all have to go. Greed and treachery, that's all it is!'

Iain watched as the people of the glen packed their belongings into panniers on their ponies' backs or carried them in bundles on their own backs. Weeping and lamenting, they made their way down the glen, leading their few cattle, pigs and dogs, some carrying a hen or two or a few ducks. They embraced each other and helped their old folk over the rough ground. A piper played, but this time it was a haunting, heart-breaking tune that made Iain almost feel like crying himself.

'"Return No More",' whispered Seamas Dhu, 'the saddest pipe lament that was ever composed.'

'But why was this allowed?' demanded Iain. 'Couldn't someone stop it?'

Seamas Dhu shook his head. 'It was allowed by those who had

the power. No one could stop it, because they didn't have the power. In my time it was so.'

Looking through the smoke, Iain could see that the glen was emptying of people. Then he saw men riding out from the castle towards the nearest crofts. He couldn't see what they were doing when they reached them, but in a few moments the thatch was ablaze and they left them burning. Iain watched in horror as they galloped down the glen, turning off to set light to every cottage, till it seemed as if every hillside was on fire. Still people struggled panic-stricken down the glen, with their pots and pans, their baskets of clothes and blankets, children and dogs and livestock.

Then Iain noticed that Seamas Dhu and his family were taking down their tents and packing up their things. 'Are you going too?' he asked.

'What else can we do?' was the reply. 'We earn our living making the things that people need. If they go away, so must we.'

'Where'll they go?'

'Down from the glen into the straths. Some of the people will be lucky, some won't. Many will go across the sea.'

'What will you do?' asked Iain. 'Will you be lucky?'

Seamas laughed bitterly. 'Who knows? We're used to travelling about to where people need us. We make and mend things, harvest crops, make music. Maybe we'll survive better than the rest. But *Gleann a' Chadail* will sleep until people come back to it again.'

Iain looked at the glen full of black smoke from the burning crofts and understood what Seamas had meant by saying a curse had come upon it.

Mairi Mor stood with her two arms raised in the air and a wild look upon her face. 'May the house of Domnall Ruraidh Mac an Dhu never thrive!' she cried in a harsh, passionate voice. 'May his heirs come to a bad end and may his line die out. May the eagle feast on their corpses and may the name of Mac an Dhu be reviled. May the treasure of the Mac an Dhus be lost until better

times come. May not one stone of his dwelling place remain above another in time to come. This is the curse of Mairi Mor!'

Iain thought he would never forget the awesome sight of Mairi Mor silhouetted against the burning glen or the sound of her terrible words. He was quite sure that there was power enough in them to bring about all that she foretold for the hapless Mac an Dhus.

'It's goodbye now, Iain Ruadh,' said Seamas Dhu. 'You must go back to your own time. But remember, you have the magic chanter. Whenever you play it, I will come.'

'Goodbye,' said Mairi Mor, in her usual gentle tones. 'Be happy, *ghille beag*.' The three children solemnly said goodbye, then the whole family picked up their bundles and started to walk down the hillside. Iain waved to them, then sat down near the place where the fire had been and felt very sad for his new friends.

Just then, Mr McFatridge appeared beside him. 'Iain!' he said crossly, 'where have you been? We've been looking everywhere for you!'

Iain looked around him in amazement. The glen with its fire and smoke and the retreating figures of Seamas Dhu's family and the rest of the departing folk had changed to the peaceful scene it had been when he played the magic chanter and all his classmates had fallen asleep. There they all were now, crowding round him and quite wide awake.

'You've all been asleep,' he said. 'But I've seen all sorts of things.'
'Like what?' demanded Neil.

'First there was a piper called Seamas Dhu. He took me to his camp and I met his wife and his children. He showed me the glen when there were people in it, and he showed me a ceilidh. Then I saw what had happened to all the people. They had to leave when they couldn't pay their rent.'

'I think it's you who's been asleep and dreaming,' said Miss Paton. 'Come on, we'll have to get a bit further up the glen before we have our mid-afternoon snack.'

'Mid-afternoon?' gasped Iain. 'But . . . '

'Don't you want anything to eat?' laughed Miss Paton. 'That's not like you, Iain! We've wasted over half an hour looking for you.'

'Half an hour? But I've been away for hours. I listened to a story that lasted all night!'

Everyone laughed and Iain realised that no one believed him. Even he couldn't explain how all that could have happened to him in such a short time.

They all began to walk up the glen once more. Fattie fell into step beside him and gave him a knowing look. 'So you've been seeing things again, have you?'

'Yes,' said Iain, and he told the teacher all that had taken place. '*You* believe me, don't you?' he pleaded.

'What you've told me fits the facts of history,' replied Fattie.

'You mean things like that did happen?'

'Oh, yes. It was called the Highland Clearances. The people were cleared off the land so that the lairds could keep sheep. That was supposed to be an improvement. Well, it may have made them richer at the time, but it was bad for the people and now it's clear that it was also bad for the land.'

Iain knitted his brows. 'I didn't think people were allowed to do that.'

Fattie smiled wryly. 'You've a lot to learn, young man.'

'Seamas Dhu said the glen would sleep until people came back to it again.'

'Well, that's pretty unlikely,' said Fattie. 'No one wants to live up a remote glen nowadays. It's too difficult. Even if someone wanted to, they couldn't afford it.'

'I think it would be great to live here,' said Iain.

'It might seem great to you in your dreams, but in reality, it'd be a nightmare. Just think, Iain, what it would cost you to travel miles to buy anything. You'd have no electricity, no running water. It'd be hard in winter – you'd probably be snowed in. You're not used to any of those things.'

'No,' he said, 'but the people I saw seemed to like it all right.'

'They had a different way of life. It was long ago. The way they lived was what they were used to. We couldn't live like that now. If they could see you, they'd think you were living in paradise.'

Iain was looking around him as they got to the place where they were going to eat. With a little tingle of excitement, he recognised the green knowe, where the old laird had introduced his son to the people of the glen as the new laird. Not far away there was a thick wood. 'That's where the castle was.'

'Well, it's not there now,' said Fattie. 'The laird's family must have died out or moved away.'

'Maybe Mairi Mor's curse worked,' said Iain.

'Maybe it did.'

Iain felt something in his pocket and pulled it out. It was the pin Seamas Dhu had given him. 'There,' he said to Fattie, 'that proves I've seen Seamas Dhu. He gave me that.'

The teacher took the pin in his hand and turned it over and over. 'It certainly looks hand-made,' he said. 'But that's impossible. It's one thing seeing things from the past. It's quite another actually to bring something back. You'd better take good care of it.'

After the picnic was over, the three teachers discussed what to do next. 'The signpost said "Inchbeg, five miles" and we've walked just over three. Is everyone ready to walk about another two?' asked Mr Lornie.

There was a chorus of 'Yes' with one or two saying 'No', just for devilment.

'You can have half an hour to explore,' said Fattie. 'See what plants, stones or other interesting things you can find. Spot any wildlife that hasn't been driven away by all the noise you're making and take some photos to show your mums and dads.'

Everybody scattered. Iain, followed by Neil, went to the top of the green knowe and looked around the glen, trying to identify where some of the crofts had been.

'Eoghan Mac an Dhu's house was up there – below that big rock,' explained Iain.

'There's nothing there now,' said Neil.

'Well, the thatch would have been burnt off it,' said Iain, 'and I expect the walls just crumbled away.'

'How big was it?' asked Neil.

'Oh, not very big. Everyone had to duck to go through the door and there weren't different rooms inside – just one big room with a sort of woven fence to mark off the bit where the cow was kept.

'They had their cows in the house?' exclaimed Neil in disbelief. 'Ugh – it must have been really smelly!'

'They didn't seem to mind. I suppose they got used to it. Anyway, there'd be the smell of smoke from the fire as well.'

'It must have been awful.'

'The ceilidh house was away down the glen. I think it was near that place where we saw two burns coming down the hillside close together.'

'What was that like – the ceilidh?'

'Oh, it was just like a get-together – a party – but everyone was there, not just the grown-ups. They weren't all dressed up. Everyone got something to eat and drink and they sang and played music and told stories all night long.'

'I went to a ceilidh once in the Salutation Hotel, but it wasn't like that. It was kind of posh and more like a concert, with a man singing and a lady playing the piano, a fiddler, a piper and some wee girl dancers.'

'There was a piper in the ceilidh house, too,' said Iain. 'He didn't play the big pipes. They're for outside. He played some smaller ones. But the best thing was the storyteller. He could tell a story that lasted all night.'

'Wow!' said Neil. 'He must have had a good memory. How could anyone remember anything as long as that?'

'It didn't seem any bother to him,' replied Iain. 'He was great! You just couldn't help listening.'

'Come on, everyone,' shouted Miss Paton. 'We'll have to be going now. Only another couple of miles to walk.'

They all came running with their plants and stones, and Fattie scribbled a list of them in his notebook.

'Right,' he said, 'you can take all these back and we'll make a table display of them in the class. I think we'll forget about the dead fieldmouse and the old tin can.'

Iain recognised the tin as another bit of Seamas's handiwork, however, so he picked it up after everyone had moved off and stuffed it in his rucksack.

They began to walk the last two miles to where they were to rejoin the bus. Many of them were now quite tired and one or two heels were blistered, but they soldiered on with a little first aid from Miss Paton's elastoplast tin. At last, they saw the bus parked down on a winding road. They were glad to climb aboard and, as they sped homeward, Iain fingered his magic chanter and wondered if he would ever again meet with Seamas Dhu or walk in *Gleann a' Chadail*, the Sleepy Glen.

6

The Visit

A few days after the hill-walk, the summer holidays began – those magical weeks with no school, no homework, and no sitting indoors when the sun was shining outside. On days when he was not going to the swimming baths or fishing down at the harbour or stravaiging about Kinnoull Hill, Iain was happy to play on the Inch with Bitsy or Neil. One afternoon as he idly kicked a ball about, he spotted old Lizzie under a tree, sitting on her heels on the grass, smoking a short clay pipe. He went over and sat beside her, but she went on puffing.

'I've never seen a lady smoke a pipe,' said Iain.

Lizzie grinned. 'I'm no lady,' she said.

'You are so.'

'Lady Muck,' she said with a chortle.

'I've been up the Sleepy Glen,' said Iain, unable to wait any longer.

'Hae ye, son?' she replied. 'And did ye faa asleep?'

'No, I didn't. Everyone else did, but I had my chanter with me.'

'Aye,' she said, 'it wad keep ye awake.'

'I met Seamas Dhu,' he said.

Lizzie's face lit up. 'I kent ye were the richt yin!' she cried with a hoarse chuckle. 'So ye'll hae a story to tell?'

'Yes,' began Iain. 'He took me up the glen and I saw it as it was long ago and . . . '

'Dinnae tell me aathin the noo,' warned Lizzie. 'Ye'll need tae come oot tae whaur I bide an tell Geordie.'

'Where's that?' asked Iain. He'd never thought of Lizzie as having a home. She just seemed to come and go like the birds or the clouds.

'Oh, I've a beautiful trailer oot at Birkenhaugh,' said Lizzie.

'I don't know where that is.'

'It's oot by Hazelburn Brig,' said Lizzie. 'Of coorse, son, ye'll no ken aboot it. It's a caravan site.'

'Oh, I see. I've seen one at St Andrews. There's hundreds of caravans on it.'

'Weel,' said Lizzie hesitantly, 'it's no quite the same. Ye see, Birkenhaugh is jist for traiveller people.'

'Why is that?'

'Weel, ye see,' said Lizzie, with a quiet smile, 'we like oor privacy jist as much as onybody else.'

'Can I come there?'

'Of coorse ye can, son.'

'But how can I get to it?'

'I tell ye whit. Ma youngest boy, Gravy, will be comin by here the morn's morn. He could pick ye up an bring ye oot.'

'What time?' asked Iain.

'Aboot twa o'clock. Is that okay, son?'

'I'll be there,' promised Iain. 'Is his name really Gravy?'

'Weel, it's whit we caa him for a by-name,' she said. 'He's Graham.'

'Does he like Gravy?'

Lizzie laughed. 'Aye he does – and ither things as weel!'

'Where'll I wait for him?'

'Jist stand in the wee lay-by whaur the bus-stop is,' said Lizzie 'Mak sure ye hae yer chanter an he'll ken ye.'

'All right,' he said.

'I'm awa noo, son,' said Lizzie getting up. 'See ye the morrow.' She walked away in the direction of the town.

Iain had to think carefully. What would he tell his mum about where he was going? He knew she wouldn't approve of his being picked up by someone neither of them knew and taken to a caravan site. He trusted Lizzie and wasn't afraid of going to visit her. In fact, he was so excited by the idea that he knew he'd never sleep that night. It would be like the night before Christmas.

As he lay in his bed, he whispered in Bitsy's ear, 'I'm going to tell Mum we're going to visit Scone Palace. She'll quite like that.'

Sure enough, Mum agreed quite readily and even gave him the entrance money. In fact, for one awful moment, he thought she was going to come with him. 'It'd be nice to see the palace again,' she said. 'I haven't been for a year or two.' Iain held his breath. 'But I'm afraid I'll have to leave it, this time. I've too much to do in the house.' Iain tried to hide his relief and ran out before she changed her mind.

At five minutes to two, he and Bitsy were standing near the bus-stop where Lizzie's son was to meet him. He held the magic chanter in his hand so that Gravy would spot him. Two o'clock came and went and so did quarter past and Iain was just about giving up and going home, when a rather battered-looking small lorry drew up beside him. Inside was a man with a shapeless felt hat stuck on the back of his mop of black hair. He leaned over, opened the passenger door and gave Iain a wide, friendly grin.

'In ye get,' he told Iain, 'your dug an aa.'

Iain clambered up into the seat and Bitsy lolloped in at his feet. Gravy banged the door shut. There was a half-eaten poke of chips on the dashboard and he pushed another warm packet into Iain's hand.

'There ye are, son. Dinnae say I'm no guid tae ye.'

'Thanks!' said Iain gratefully. He loved to eat chips out of the bag, but Mum never liked him to do that. Not when he was with her at any rate.

'Ye're riding on the Gravy Train!' said Gravy with a wink. In the back of the lorry, there was a lot of rattling.

'What's that noise?' asked Iain.

'Just some scrap I'm takin tae Heggie's yaird.' Iain knew that was beside the station and he'd often stared over the wall at the piles of old cars and many completely unidentifiable pieces of twisted metal that lay there.

'Why are you taking it there?'

Gravy laughed. 'Jist for fun, wee man, jist for fun!'

Iain looked puzzled. Gravy roared with laughter again, then said, suddenly serious, 'It's ma livin.'

'How's it your living?'

'Well, I gaither up aa the scrap, aa the stuff fowk doesnae want, and I sells it tae auld Heggie.'

'Why on earth does he want to buy it?'

'Because it's valuable. A lot o it can be re-used.'

'Do you get much for it?'

'That depends. Some bits are worth a lot. Some's worth nothin.'

'What about this lot?'

'Och, I'll get a few pounds, son. No enough for a hol'day in Spain, but enough tae fill ma belly.'

They drew up at the scrapyard and Gravy got out to unload. Old Mr Heggie in dirty overalls came out of his ramshackle office to watch.

'Whit ye got the day, then?' he asked at last.

'Jist wait till ye see this,' Gravy shouted from the back of the lorry. He hauled off something heavy and laid it on the ground.

Mr Heggie peered at it as if his sight was poor. 'What is it?' he demanded.

'It's the propeller aff a jet airliner,' said Gravy. 'Ye'll no see twa o them in the wan year.'

'It's mair like the landing wheel aff a hovercraft,' said Mr Heggie. They thumped each other on the back and burst out laughing. They obviously had a game of seeing who could make up the daftest patter. Iain had no idea what the assorted lumps of metal were, but Mr Heggie must have known, for he nodded agreement and paid Gravy from a grubby wad of notes he took out of his back pocket.

Gravy climbed back into the driver's seat and drove away whistling cheerfully. Iain recognised a pipe tune Seamas Dhu had played and asked, 'Do *you* play the pipes?'

Gravy grinned. 'Aye,' he said, 'aa the family does. We're kent for that.'

'I saw your father at the shows on the Inch. Does he often do that?'

'Oh aye,' replied Gravy, 'specially in the summer. He gaes up tae Glencoe an he plays for aa the gentry there on hol'day.'

'Is he there now?'

'Weel, he was, but he'd tae come doon tae Perth for a fun'ral yesterday.'

'Whose funeral was it?'

'It was one o his uncles, an auld man o echty-seiven.'

'How many uncles does he have?' asked Iain, amazed to think of Geordie having an uncle at all.

'Oh aboot twelve,' replied Gravy calmly.

'Twelve!' Iain was hardly able to believe his ears. 'He must have an awful lot of cousins then.'

'Hunners,' said Gravy. 'He's got six brithers and five sisters an aa. Ma has fower brithers and three sisters. So I hae hunners o cousins tae. Then there's ma brithers an sisters. There's Geordie, but we caa him Deeks, Ji, Annie, Isy, Motor Man – that's Jimmy – and me.'

'Just like a clan!' said Iain.

'Of coorse,' said Gravy. 'That's whit we are, son. So there's plenty o fun'rals – an sometimes weddins!'

He laughed long and loud at this so Iain asked, 'Do you like those?'

'Oh aye,' said Gravy, 'it's aa great crack! Great crack!'

'Crack?' echoed Iain, vaguely remembering something he'd seen on television. 'Is that not some awful drug?'

Gravy roared with laughter again. 'No, no, baby. Whit I mean is – och, just the haill lot o us gettin thegither. Fun'rals is best, cause there's the wake.'

'What's that?' asked Iain.

'We stey up for three nichts. That's the wake.'

'What do you do? Just stay up?'

'No, no. There's aye freens comin tae pey their respects. There's tea for aab'dy – an booze, of coorse. Och, ye hear some stories at a wake, an sangs, an tunes.'

'Sounds like a ceilidh to me,' said Iain.

'An whit dae ye ken o ceilidhs, wee man?'

Iain kept quiet. He wondered if Gravy would believe his story of the Sleepy Glen and Seamas Dhu.

They were now rattling along a country road that led away from the outskirts of the town. At last, they turned into a wide entrance that brought them into an area in which a large number of big modern caravan trailers were arranged like a village, where children played and dogs lay in the sun. Gravy drove up to one of the trailers and stopped.

'Here we are noo,' he said.

The door of the trailer opened and out came old Lizzie, smiling broadly. She gave Iain and Bitsy a warm welcome and took them into the trailer, while Gravy opened up the bonnet of the lorry and began to inspect the engine. 'I'll no be minutes, Ma,' he said. 'I'll jist hae a look at ma distributor.'

'Here y'are, Geordie,' Lizzie was saying. 'Here's the man himsel!'

Geordie was sitting on one of the long seats at the far end of the trailer, wearing an old felt hat, a worn-looking jumper, brown cords and stout boots. In his hand was a pipe chanter and, on a ledge beside him, a mug of tea. At his feet lay a small terrier which sprang up and welcomed Bitsy.

'Come awa in,' Geordie called. 'Ye're a sicht for sair een.'

Iain looked around him and was fascinated by what he saw. What he had expected he couldn't have said, but it was nothing like this. White lace screens and bright-coloured curtains and cushions, photographs and pictures, and fine china and brass ornaments made the inside of the trailer so cheerful and welcoming. Bitsy immediately curled up in a snug corner as if to say, 'I like it here.' Lizzie, in a red-checked shawl over a bright blue dress, sat smiling in the midst of a mass of gorgeous flowers. Iain hadn't noticed any gardens on the site, apart from plants in boxes or pots. But then he remembered the day at the shows and the basket of flowers Lizzie had had then.

'Where did you say these flowers came from?' he asked.

'These is widden flooers, son,' she replied. 'I mak them.' Sure enough, she was paring the end of a long thin stick with a sharp knife, so that the ends curled over like chrysanthemum petals. It looked so easy!

'What kind of wood is it?' Iain asked.

'It's bourtree,' Lizzie answered, 'whit ye wad caa the elder tree.'

'I see ye've brocht yer chanter,' said Geordie. 'Come on, noo, and gie's a tune on it.'

Iain wasn't sure if the magic would work here, but he put the pipe to his lips and fingered the stops. Sure enough, it began to play.

'Hey!' cried Geordie when he had finished. 'Whaur did ye learn tae play like that, wee man?'

'Well, I didn't,' said Iain, feeling his face grow red. 'It just does it by itself.'

Geordie slapped his knees delightedly and crowed in triumph. 'That's richt! That's richt! It's the magic chanter, sure enough. That's hoo ye were able tae see the Sleepy Glen. And did it keep ye awake?'

'Oh yes,' said Iain. 'I met Seamas Dhu and he showed me what the glen used to be like in his time and what happened to the people.'

Geordie stared at Iain, with his large, dark eyes blazing with excitement. 'Seamas Dhu was ma grandfaither's grandfaither!' he shouted. 'That was *his* chanter.'

'You look like him,' cried Iain. 'You really do!' Geordie didn't have long hair or a beard but you could see the resemblance in his features. Iain couldn't have said anything that would have pleased big Geordie more.

'Sit doon by me, son, and I'll learn ye anither tune,' he said. He put his chanter to his lips and broke into a march tune.

'What's that?' asked Iain when he'd finished.

'Thon's ma ain tune,' said Geordie. 'Geordie Blackie's March. Try it wi me.'

Iain lifted his magic chanter and played along with Geordie, while Lizzie beamed at them as she made her flowers.

'Noo,' said Geordie when they had played the tune several times, 'tell me aa yer crack aboot Seamas Dhu.'

So with Bitsy at his feet, Iain told them the whole of his adventures in the Sleepy Glen. They listened to every word intently, never taking their eyes from his face. When he got to the end of his story, they each gave a long, appreciative sigh.

'That's quite a tale, wee man,' said Geordie. Lizzie got up and busied herself putting on the kettle and laying out fine china cups and saucers with roses on them.

'Geordie,' said Iain, 'can I ask you something?'

'Ask awa, son,' said Geordie. 'I'm no whit ye'd caa an educated man, but maybe I'm somethin better.'

'Maybe you are,' said Iain.

Geordie leaned over and looked right in to his eyes. 'I'm traiveller-brained,' he said, with a knowing smile. 'Aye one jump ahead o the country hantle.'

'What kind of handle?'

'No handle – hantle!'

'What's that?'

Geordie laughed. 'That's aa the fowk that arenae traivellers. Them that live settled.'

'Am I country hantle?'

Geordie looked at him hard. 'I'm no shair that ye are, son. Ye're wi the gift. Ye're mair like ane o us.'

Iain knew this was meant as a compliment and it pleased him. Lizzie gave him a cup of tea and a big roll filled with ham. 'There ye are, baby.'

Gravy came into the trailer and sat down to have tea with them. 'Whit was it ye wanted tae ask me?' Geordie inquired.

'Oh – I nearly forgot,' said Iain with a laugh, 'talking about hantle. I was wondering if you knew why I can see all these things.'

'I cannae tell ye that, son,' he replied. 'That's whit ye caa a mystery. Life's fu o mysteries. Ye jist have tae accept them.'

'Do you think,' asked Iain, 'that maybe it's so's I can tell people what things were really like long ago?'

'Mebbe,' said Geordie. 'Aye, mebbe that's it.' He took time to light his pipe. 'Ye see, son, nooadays fowk dinnae ken aboot lang syne. They dinnae want tae ken. They think it disnae maitter.'

Lizzie nodded. 'We can see that, son. We see it wi aa the fowk we go aboot. They're no like us.'

'Do you know about long ago?'

'Oh aye,' said Lizzie. 'We aa ken wha we're frae, wha oor past generations were. We've stories and sangs handed doon for hunners o years.'

'Aa that ye tellt us aboot Seamas Dhu,' said Geordie, 'we kent aa ready.'

Iain was flabbergasted. 'You knew?'

'Da tellt me aboot Seamas Dhu when I was younger than you,' said Gravy.

'Where did he go after he left the Sleepy Glen?' Iain felt a whole series of questions starting up in his head. 'Was he lucky? Did he find a way to make a living? How did his family get on? Did they all stay together? Did he go on making baskets?'

'Haud yer horses,' begged Geordie, laughing. 'I cannae gie ye aa the answers. I think he got on gey weel, better than a lot o the fairmin fowk wha lost their land. He was kent as a guid piper an he aye had camps aa owre the place. He used tae camp aroon Birnam and roon by Alyth.'

Iain felt very strange as he realised that Seamas Dhu, who seemed to him like a figure in a dream, that no one had seen but himself, was a real person, a real ancestor of Geordie Blackie.

'How is your name Geordie Blackie,' he asked, 'when his was Seamas Dhu?'

'*Dhu* is from a Gaelic word,' Geordie said. 'It means "black". When the people stopped using the Gaelic, they started cryin us Blackie insteid o Mac an Dhu.'

'Have you ever been to the Sleepy Glen?'

'No, but we can dae that, noo ye're here.'

'How's that?'

'Ye hae the magic chanter.'

'But you gave me it. Why couldn't *you* go with it?'

'It had tae be played by the richt yin. The yin wha can bring the fowk back tae the glen.'

'Is that me?'

'It must be, son, it must be.'

'But why me?'

Geordie laughed. 'That's anither mystery for ye! Look at it this wey. Why no?'

'What have I to do?' asked Iain.

'Nuthin,' said Geordie. 'Jist ye awa hame an wait an see whit happens. It'll aa turn oot the wey it's meant tae.'

Iain looked at his watch. 'Oh, Jeronimo!' he cried. 'Look at the time! I'll have to get home.'

'Dinna fash, son,' said Gravy. 'I'll tak ye hame.'

'Just anither tune, son,' said Geordie.

They took up their chanters and played together. 'I'd like to really learn the pipes,' said Iain, 'not just play them the magic way. Can you teach me, Geordie?'

'Shairly,' said Geordie. 'Awa wi ye, noo. I'm awa back up the glen the morn. I'll see ye when I see ye.' He and Lizzie shook Iain warmly by the hand and Lizzie gave him a sprig of white heather – 'for luck'.

Soon he and Bitsy were speeding back into Perth, this time in a rather rattly small car, which Gravy drove quite fast. 'What'll you do now?'

'I'm goin tae meet ma brither, Ji, in the pub,' said Gravy.

Remembering the time he saw Geordie and Lizzie at the shows, Iain said, 'Dinna come back peevie.'

Gravy nearly drove the car into a lamp post and drew up with a screech of brakes. 'Whaur did ye hear that?' he yelled, choking with laughter.

'I heard your mother say it to your father at the shows.'

Gravy chortled and chuckled helplessly over the steering wheel. 'My, ye must be a traiveller richt enough tae mang the cant like that!'

'What's that?'

'We've got words we use – oor ain words. "Peevie" – that's drunk. If ye mang the cant, ye speak like a traiveller.'

'Does your father get drunk?'

'Aye, sometimes. Does yours?'

'Only at Hogmanay,' said Iain. 'Do you mind me using your words – mangin the cant?'

'Naw, naw. Ye're a freen.'

'Am I? Honest?'

'Sure ye are. On ma mither's grave.'

'Your mother's not dead!' laughed Iain.

'Neither she is,' Gravy stopped laughing. 'I shouldnae hae said that. Mak it ma grandmither's grave.' They both burst out laughing again. 'We shouldnae laugh,' Gravy told him. 'It's no respectfu. If ye sweer on someb'dy's grave it's deid serious. Ye hae tae mean it.'

They were back at the Inch again, so Iain got out with Bitsy.

'See ye again soon, son!' Gravy waved cheerily and drove off. Iain walked along to his gate, hoping his mother wouldn't ask too many questions about his visit to Scone Palace.

7

A Vision of the Future

It was a week or two after his visit to Geordie and Lizzie that Iain's dad called him into the sitting-room. He had a big map spread out on the coffee table and was looking at it closely through a magnifying glass.

'I was just trying to find that glen you said you did the hill-walk in,' he said.

'It wasn't *on* the map,' Iain reminded him. 'Mr McFatridge and Mr Lornie couldn't find it.'

'Maybe they didn't have such a detailed map as this,' said Mr Barlass. 'It must be on the map if it was there and you walked in it.'

'Well,' began Iain, 'it was . . . ' He didn't know how to explain it to his dad.

'It was what?' asked Dad in amusement, 'Brigadoon? Atlantis?'

'What are they?'

'Oh, just storybook places that are supposed to appear and disappear.'

'Yes!' said Iain. 'That's what it is!'

'Now, come on, son,' protested Dad, 'you're nine years old now. You're too big to believe in fairytales!'

'But it's true,' insisted Iain. 'It was only because I had the magic chanter with me that it was there.'

'Magic chanter!' Iain's dad laid down the magnifying glass and looked at his son as if he had suddenly sprouted horns. 'What are you talking about? What's all this nonsense?' He was beginning to look annoyed.

'It isn't nonsense, Dad, honest! It's true. I know it sounds funny, but you've got to believe me. I wouldn't tell you lies.'

'I should think not!'

'You see, I can see things from long ago. I had the magic chanter and I was able to see the glen the way it was at one time.'

'Where did you get this magic chanter?' Dad was almost laughing at him now.

'Lizzie Blackie gave me it. It belonged to Seamas Dhu. He was a sort of ancestor of hers.' Iain went on to tell his father all about Seamas Dhu and his adventure in the Sleepy Glen.

Dad put his arm round Iain's shoulder and began to laugh out loud. 'So *that's* where all this is from. Lizzie Blackie! That's who's been filling your head with all these havers.'

'No, it's not! I saw things long before I talked to her,' Iain told him hotly.

'Listen, son!' Dad held him gently by the shoulders and looked earnestly at him. 'You've always had a good imagination. There's nothing wrong with that. But you mustn't pay any attention to the stories of a traveller woman. She's a dear old soul and quite harmless, I know, but she doesn't know the difference between truth and fantasy.'

'Do you?' demanded Iain. 'Maybe there isn't all that much difference.'

'That's an odd thing to say!'

'Well, you said it's fantasy when I talk about Seamas Dhu. But he was a real person. And what he told me about what happened in the Sleepy Glen did happen. Mr McFatridge said so.'

'Oh,' said Dad in a mocking tone, 'of course, if Mr McFatridge says so, it must be true.'

'Well, it's in the history books. That's not fantasy!'

'I'm sure you read your history book well,' said Dad. 'You're a bright wee lad. And, of course, it's a good thing to try and picture the things you've read about.'

'But I haven't read about them yet,' said Iain. 'It was Mr

McFatridge who knew about the . . . the Clearances. He said things like that *had* happened when I told him what I'd seen.'

'He believed you?'

'Yes. he did.'

Dad said nothing but rubbed his chin with his finger and thumb.

'Don't *you* believe me, Dad?'

His father looked thoughtful. 'Maybe I'd better have a word with Mr McFatridge,' he said. School wasn't due to start for a week or two yet, for which Iain felt quite glad. He wasn't sure that he wanted his father to talk to Fattie.

'I tell you what,' said Dad, 'tomorrow's Saturday. Let's go for a run up to Glenisla – we'll see if we can find your Sleepy Glen.'

'All right, Dad!' Iain was elated.

'Be sure and bring your magic chanter!' laughed Dad as Iain went out of the room to go and tell Bitsy.

'You can come too, Bitsy. We'll maybe see Seamas Dhu again.'

The next day was very warm and sunny; the perfect day for a trip to Glenisla. Mum and Dad put a picnic basket in the car early in the morning and they set off along the beautiful Isla Road to Blairgowrie. They travelled through the many lovely vistas and past numerous magnificent old trees spreading out their branches beside golden fields of grain; past the berryfields that were world famous. The berry harvest was nearly over but there were still some pickers at work.

'When I was a girl,' said Mum, 'everyone went to the berries.'

'How did you go?' asked Iain.

'Some went in buses, others went on the backs of lorries. We usually sang all the way. What a lot of fun we had!'

'Why don't so many people go now?'

'I don't know. Maybe they don't need the money.'

'You got money for picking berries?'

'Oh yes! That's why a lot of people went. Many of them needed the money to buy clothes and shoes for the winter.'

'How much did you get?'

'Oh, it varied. Just a few pence a pound. Old pennies, that was. You had to pick a lot to make it worthwhile.'

As she spoke, they were driving past a berryfield with a large notice that said, 'Pick your own rasps and straws, 30p a pound.'

'Changed days,' said Dad. 'Now you pay to pick!'

'But you get the berries,' pointed out Mrs Barlass.

'The farmer gets his crop picked and sold at one go. Changed days, as I said.'

Soon they were threading their way through the narrow hilly streets of Blairgowrie and out on the road to Alyth, which went up and down like a switchback. Once through Alyth, though, the Angus braes spread before them, and then Glenisla.

'Now, the bus dropped you at Ardbeth,' said Dad, drawing up by the roadside and spreading the map on the dashboard.

'That's right,' said Iain.

'Hmm, that's just a couple of miles further on.'

They drove on slowly along the winding road with hills on each side. Ardbeth was just a few houses, a clachan rather than a village. Just beyond it was a signpost.

'That's it!' said Iain.

They drew up again and his father got out with the map in his hand and went up to look at the signpost. It was old and worn but plainly said, 'Inchbeg, five miles,' and pointed up the little steep side road Iain remembered.

'That's funny,' said Dad. 'There shouldn't be a road here at all.'

'Well, there is,' said Iain, 'and it's the road to the Sleepy Glen.'

'I'm not taking the car up there,' said Dad. 'It's hardly more than a track.'

They parked the car and took out the picnic basket to carry with them. Iain whistled to Bitsy who ran ahead chasing rabbits – real and imaginary – while Iain followed with the magic chanter in his hand. Once they were a good bit up the road, he put it to his lips and began to play. Mum and Dad couldn't believe their ears.

'My goodness! Where did you learn to play like that?'

'I didn't!' said Iain.

'What do you mean?' said Mum. 'You're playing, so you must've learned to play.'

'No, Mum, honest,' said Iain. 'It's the magic, you see.'

Mum and Dad looked at each other and shrugged their shoulders, laughing. It was too sunny a day for arguments. Iain walked on ahead with Bitsy, still playing. He came to a large rock and climbed on to the top of it, imagining himself with a full set of pipes; a lone piper on the ramparts of a castle. At last, he stopped playing and looked down the glen road to see if Mum and Dad were coming. They were sitting in the shade of a birch tree fast asleep.

He slid down the side of the rock, followed closely by Bitsy, and wandered further up, past trailing bushes of brambles. A few were quite black and juicy-looking so he picked and ate them.

'In a week or two's time, you'll be able to fill a basket,' said a voice behind him. He turned to find Seamas Dhu with a bundle of willow wands slung on his back.

'Hallo!' cried Iain. 'I've come back and Mum and Dad are with me this time.'

'I know,' said Seamas. 'That's why you'll see the glen in your time, not in mine. You'll see the ruined cottages, the remaining walls of the kirk, the old mill wheel, the big house derelict.'

'Will they meet you?'

'I think not.'

'But they don't believe me when I talk about you,' protested Iain. 'They think I've made you up. You must let them see you're really here, not just something I've imagined.'

'Why shouldn't I be that?'

'But if I just imagine I can see you, that means you're not really here!'

'Does it?' Seamas sat down on a moss-covered stone. 'Now, just listen to me, *mo ghille ruadh*. It is with your imagination that you see into the past and the future. You see what has been and you see what is to come.'

Iain put his hand on Seamas Dhu's arm. 'But you are here. I can feel your shirt and your arm inside it. You're real.'

'Yes,' laughed Seamas. 'Strange, isn't it? How do you explain it?'

'It's magic.'

Seamas looked at him seriously. 'As long as you can believe that, you hold the secret of life,' he said. He rose and lifted his bundle of wands. 'The world is full of magic,' he shouted as he strode away up the glen.

Iain felt disappointed to see him go. 'I wish he'd stay,' he said to Bitsy. Magic people seemed so unpredictable. Looking back, he saw Mum and Dad coming slowly up the path towards him. Bitsy ran to meet them barking excitedly as if to say, 'You should see what we've seen!'

'Well, Iain, are you going to show us round this Sleepy Glen of yours?' asked Dad as they drew near.

'We're coming to some of the places I saw,' said Iain. 'At least, what's left of them. Look, there's where the mill was. There's only the mill wheel now. That cottage up there was Eoghan Mac an Dhu's. He had great knowledge of medicine and he could tell stories that lasted all night.'

His father looked surprised. 'You seem very sure of yourself,' he said.

'Away up there – see? – that's what's left of the kirk.'

They walked on a good bit further. 'Over there,' said Iain pointing, 'that was the house where they had all the ceilidhs. That was Aonghas Mac an Dhu's. There's only one wall left now.'

'You're making this up, Iain!' cried Mum.

'No I'm not. Do you see that wood away ahead?'

They shaded their eyes. 'Yes.'

'Well, in that wood you'll find what's left of the big house.'

'We'll see,' said Dad. It took them nearly half an hour to reach the trees. Iain and Dad and Bitsy could hardly find the path through the wood, so overgrown as it was with brambles and bracken and gorse. Mum stayed behind to get the food ready, and Iain waved to her as she watched them disappear into the wood.

At length, Iain and his dad struggled through, beating a path with sticks, until they came upon a tall piece of stone, covered in moss and half sunk in a bed of giant thistles. Iain's father took a stick and beat a passage through the thistles to it. He scraped at the moss until suddenly, there, carved in the stone, was revealed the name Mac an Dhu!

'That must be one of the door pillars or gate pillars,' said Iain. 'But where's the house?'

'Remember I told you Mairi Mor put a curse on it. She said, "May there be not one stone of it left upon another." Looks as if it's come true.'

Sure enough, at a distance from the carved stone, with Bitsy's help they found a few crumbling slabs in the undergrowth.

'Yes,' agreed Dad, 'that must have been a pretty efficient curse. A cottage could disappear altogether through time, but a big house should stand longer.'

This was the first real sign Dad had given of believing anything Iain had told him.

'Who did it belong to?'

'Domnall Ruraidh Mac an Dhu,' replied Iain promptly. 'His family had lived there a long time. It was his son who drove the people out.'

Just then they heard Mum calling through the wood. 'Iain! Jim! Are you there? Come and eat!' They found her sitting under a big rowan tree with the contents of the picnic basket spread on a checked cloth. It was an ideal spot, shaded but looking out over the sunlit glen.

'Rowan trees are supposed to be lucky,' said Mum. 'My granny used to make charms with rowan berries and red thread to keep us safe from witches.'

'Sounds as if she was a witch herself,' said Iain.

As they tucked into corned beef sandwiches, crusty salad rolls and slabs of fruit cake, Dad asked, 'What about this Seamas Dhu? Do we get to see him as well?'

'I don't think so,' said Iain. 'He was here when you were asleep, but he went away again.'

'We weren't asleep, were we?' exclaimed Dad.

'You were,' retorted Iain. 'When I was playing my chanter, you fell asleep. It's . . . part of the magic, I think.'

'Magic!' scoffed Dad, but not quite so scornfully as before. It was as if he was trying to convince himself it was nonsense.

'Play your chanter again,' said Mum, 'and see what happens.'

Iain took it from his rucksack and started to play. In a few moments, his mum and dad were fast asleep and out from behind the rowan tree stepped Seamas Dhu.

'You've done well, Iain Beag,' he said. 'You've remembered the right things and you've spoken of them well. Do you think they believe you now?'

'I'm sure they'd believe me if only you'd let them see you.'

'I'll do better than that. I'll let them see what the future could hold.'

'What do you mean?'

'I'll show them the glen as it could be in years to come.'

'But why?'

'Oh, let's just say, to give their imagination something to work on,' said Seamas.

'How will you do that?'

'Just watch!'

As Iain watched, a white haar came creeping up the glen until everything – hills, rocks, path, trees, ruins – had disappeared into it. Eventually it swirled round the towering form of Seamas Dhu, Bitsy and Iain, and his mum and dad as they sat sleeping. They all faded away into the enveloping mist. Iain could hear a muffled booming sound, growing louder and louder until he felt he was inside some giant loudspeaker.

'What's happening?' he cried in alarm.

'Don't be afraid!' shouted Seamas Dhu. 'It's harder to get into the future than into the past.'

The booming sound began to die down and the haar started to roll back to reveal a scene that made Iain gasp in amazement.

A fine new road wound up the glen which was now thickly studded with pleasant stone and timber houses, shaped to follow the lines of the hillside, surrounded by lots of trees of every kind, parks with deer and other livestock and a loch with boats. There were heli-pads on the rocky hill shoulders, girdled with greenery and with small 'copters parked on some of them, like pretty insects. Most striking of all was that everywhere you looked, there were people working, walking about, fishing, driving, sitting on terraces, riding. The mill seemed to be working again, its waterwheel turning with a cheerful clatter. There were buildings which were not noticeable at first because they blended into the hillsides so well and looked as if they were part of the landscape.

Iain looked round to ask Seamas Dhu about them and found his mum and dad were awake and looking at it all with the same astonishment as himself.

'Where did all this come from?' asked Dad, scrambling to his feet. He gazed round at the transformation in utter bewilderment.

'It's the future,' said Iain.

'I must be dreaming,' said Mum.

'We all have to dream,' said a voice from behind the tree. Seamas Dhu stepped forward and handed her a small basket of brambles.

'That's Seamas Dhu!' whispered Iain, so glad that he had at last shown himself.

'We all have to dream,' said Seamas again. 'First the dream, then the reality.'

'I've always thought it was the other way round,' said Dad.

'What are those buildings over there?' asked Iain. 'The ones that look as if they're part of the hillside.'

'Oh,' said Seamas carelessly, 'it doesn't matter what they are. What you must remember is that they were built like that, to look natural.'

'What do you mean?' asked Iain.

'I think *I* know,' said Dad. 'You see, it's got something to do with my job,' he explained.

'I know,' said Seamas, waving his arm towards the view before them. 'Take a good look,' he said, 'and maybe you'll learn something useful.'

Iain's dad looked long and hard at the strange buildings. The stone of their walls was the stone of the glen, but that and the timbers of the doors and windows were fashioned in such a way that they harmonised with the hawthorn, heather and whin that surrounded them, so that it was impossible to tell where the trees and plants ended and the buildings began.

As they looked, Iain became aware that the white mist was creeping back over everything and slowly it all disappeared.

'Seamas Dhu,' began Iain, but when he turned, his friend had gone again.

'Unbelievable!' said Dad.

'How can you say that?' demanded Iain. 'You've just seen it for yourself!'

The haar swirled round them, chilling them, and the booming echo grew louder and louder. Bitsy cuddled in against Iain's right leg until the noise faded away and the sunlight returned. They were back in the Sleepy Glen of Iain's time, with its bare hillsides and scattered ruins.

'Time to go home,' said Dad. They started to walk down the glen to where they had parked the car.

'What are we going to do now, Dad?'

'I don't know,' said Dad, 'but we'll have to do something. For the time being, however, keep this quiet.'

'Trust me,' said Iain.

8

The Hidden Parchment

In the days that followed the picnic, Iain's house had a series of mysterious visitors. They came in the evening when his father was home from work and they spent a long time in the sitting-room talking. When Iain asked what was going on, Dad said, 'Oh, it's just something to do with my work.' He was a partner in a firm of architects. Iain thought no more about it, and certainly didn't connect it with what had happened in the Sleepy Glen.

Then one night he answered the doorbell and found Fattie on the doorstep. He was carrying a small hold-all.

'Oh,' said Iain. 'Hallo, Mr McFatridge. Is it me you've come to see?'

'Well, not exactly. Your father phoned me. He says you've been back to the glen.'

'Yes,' said Iain. 'Did he tell you about it?'

'He told me a little.'

Dad came along the hall. 'Come in,' he said. As they moved into the sitting-room, he put a hand on Iain's shoulder. 'You run along just now, Iain.'

'But . . . ' began Iain indignantly.

'You can come in later,' he said. 'I want to talk to Mr McFatridge first.'

Iain turned to appeal to his teacher. 'Do what your Dad says,' Fattie advised him. 'We can all talk together in a wee while.'

'All right,' said Iain. 'Come on, Bitsy. Let's go upstairs and play Subbuteo!'

'Subbuteo?' laughed Fattie. 'That's a blast from the past!'

'It was Dad's and he gave it to me,' Iain explained.

'A family tradition, eh? So, you play it with your dog?'

'He sometimes wins!' declared Iain.

Dad and Fattie laughed heartily as they closed the sitting-room door. Iain ran noisily up the stairs, then tiptoed down and stationed himself close to the door. He could hear every word spoken inside. He heard Dad tell Fattie of their visit to the Sleepy Glen.

'I don't know if you can believe this,' Dad began with a slightly nervous laugh. 'I found it hard to believe myself. I mean, this is the twentieth century.'

Iain wished his father could have let *him* tell the story. He could have told him there was no need to fear that Fattie wouldn't believe him.

'Well,' said Fattie afterwards, 'it certainly is very strange, one could almost say far-fetched. Iain has told me about other odd experiences, too. He's a very unusual boy in some ways, and we have to be very careful about these things.'

Iain was amazed to hear his teacher sound so cagey. 'Maybe he thinks Dad doesn't believe it and doesn't want to sound as if *he* does. Why do they have to pretend they don't believe it, when they really do?' Grown-ups seemed to play such complicated games with one another. They always seemed to be so afraid that other people might think they were not very clever.

The two men went on for quite a bit in this vein, saying things that began with, 'Maybe you think this is a lot of nonsense,' or, 'I don't want to seem over-credulous,' until gradually they began to realise that they both shared the same point of view. Then Iain heard his dad say,

'It's given me a wild idea that I've been airing to a few people.'

'What's that?' asked Mr McFatridge.

'Well, basically it's about how to bring that glen back to life.'

'I've been thinking about that too. Have you any notion where to begin?'

'Not a clue. But there must be some way. Trouble is, whatever was done, it'd need a lot of cash.'

Iain could tell by the tone of their voices that they were now on to the subject that they really wanted to talk about.

'Where to begin!' Dad sounded quite excited. 'I've had quite a few ideas, but none of them sounds quite right. First, there's the tourist thing – you know what I mean? A heritage centre or a sports complex. Wooden chalets, or a time-share place if you want to be up-market, caravan parks. But that's not really bringing the glen back to life – it's turning it into a museum piece or a playground for strangers.'

'I agree,' said Fattie warmly. 'It's no use just making it into a holiday resort. We need people to come and live and work there.'

'We have to find things that will draw people back.'

'Would you like to look at what I've got in this bag?'

Iain wished he could see through the door. Even through the keyhole, he couldn't see anything, because the two men were not sitting in front of it. He fairly fumed with frustration.

'What's all this?' he heard Dad ask.

'Oh, just some of the weird and wonderful things the children collected in the glen. We made a table display in the classroom with them.'

Iain racked his brains to try and remember what there had been on the table, but he couldn't. At the time, he'd thought it a fairly uninspiring collection and hadn't taken much notice.

'What's this?' asked Dad. 'It looks like a withered plant.'

'That's camomile,' said Mr McFatridge. 'It's a herb used in natural medicine. It's also good for the skin and hair – just the sort of thing people are turning to these days. You know, the Green Party and all that stuff about saving the planet by using natural substances instead of chemicals.'

Iain was beginning to find this very boring; what had herbs to do with bringing the glen back to life?

To his surprise, his father responded with enthusiasm. 'Good heavens! You could grow hundreds of acres of that sort of thing in the glen! All kinds of herbs! It's the up and coming thing. My sister-in-law in Edinburgh runs some kind of health and body shop. All their stuff comes from plants and herbs.'

The first time Iain had heard about his Aunt Margo's shop, he was a bit bemused. What on earth was a 'body shop'? He'd had a daft vision of a shop lined with shelves stacked with people or parts of bodies. He knew now what it really was, of course, but he giggled just the same.

'Well, it's an idea,' said Fattie, 'but it'd hardly be enough. Anyway, the herbs have to be processed to make lotions and creams and things like that.'

'Oh, I'm sure we'll need several different things,' agreed Dad.

'Here's something else,' said Fattie. 'It's a ring. When I first saw it, it was all coated with dirt and tarnished, but it's solid silver.'

'Do you think there's more like it up there?' asked Dad.

'Well, there could be. I think we'll have to check that out with Seamas Dhu. He's the one who could tell us. After all, it may've been he who made the ring.'

'You're quite sure he exists?'

'Well, whether he exists or not, Iain's got a lot of information from him,' pointed out Fattie, 'information that he couldn't have known himself, but which is true. I've never met him, of course.'

'I have,' admitted Dad, 'and he's definitely there. Either that or I'm suffering from delusions.'

'Maybe we'll all end up in the Murray Royal,' chuckled Fattie. 'When we start talking to other people, they'll think we've gone bonkers.'

'There's one or two I've talked to already who think that!' laughed Dad. 'Not to worry! We'll convince them yet.'

Iain wondered who the people were who thought his dad had gone crazy. He'd like to talk to them and take them up the Sleepy Glen. They wouldn't make a fool of his dad then.

'Have you anything else in your bag?'

'Quite a few things. There's a feather from a bird that's now very rare here – the osprey or fish-eagle. If people thought there were ospreys in the glen, you'd get all the ornithologists and nature lovers of the day.'

'What's that bit of horn?'

'This, I think, is the most interesting thing of all. Not the horn itself – it's from a stag's antler – but what's inside it.'

There was a long pause, during which Iain fairly burned with curiosity to know what was happening. If only he could see through the door! He felt like bursting into the room, but he contained himself and went on listening.

'Look at this,' he heard Fattie say at last. 'It was rolled up tight and tucked inside the horn. It must've been hollowed out to make a hiding place for it. It seems to be a kind of parchment or linen – very flimsy. I'm almost scared to touch it.'

'That's amazing!'

'There's writing on it – in Gaelic, of course.'

'Do you know what it says?'

'I asked my friend, Murdo Mackenzie, about it and he wrote me a translation. I've got it here.'

'Read it out loud!' begged Iain under his breath. He heard his father read it once in an undertone but he couldn't make out what he said. He nearly banged his head on the wall with rage, but then heard Fattie repeat it more audibly. Thank goodness he had a teacher's habit of reading slowly and clearly.

'Hidden by water, darkened by sunrise, defended by the hunter, the treasure of the Mac an Dhu.'

At the word 'treasure', Iain's heart leapt. Here, at last, was something exciting! He fairly danced and Bitsy, who'd been crouching beside him, uttered a short, shrill yelp. Suddenly, the door opened and Dad stood there trying to look angry.

'Have you been listening at the keyhole, you rascal?' he demanded sternly, but his eyes were twinkling.

'I'm sorry, Dad,' Iain said, trying to look it. 'I couldn't help it.

I just had to know what was going on. Are we going to look for the treasure?'

Both men laughed heartily. 'That's right!' said Fattie.

'Where would we start?' asked Dad.

'Seamas Dhu would know,' said Iain confidently.

'Don't get carried away, Iain,' advised Fattie. 'It's too story-bookish. What do you think you're going to find, even if you knew where to look? A crock of gold? A chest full of diamonds?'

'Maybe swords and daggers or a shield,' suggested Iain.

'What would a Highland clan regard as a treasure? It might be very different from anything we would imagine.'

'Whatever it was,' said Iain, 'it must've been important.'

'You're right,' said Fattie. 'Look how carefully these lines were written on this bit of parchment and hidden away so dry and safe. Perhaps the chief or laird carried this piece of horn in his sporran. It's small enough.'

Iain looked at the piece of horn and suddenly remembered the scene on the green knowe, when old Domnall Ruraidh Mac an Dhu had addressed his people. Round his neck had hung a piece of horn just like this!

'Let me see it,' he said eagerly. Sure enough, at one end there was a small hole through which a chain or thong could have passed. 'I've seen this before!' he cried. 'I saw old Domnall Ruraidh Mac an Dhu with it round his neck.'

The two men looked at each other. 'Are you sure?' asked Dad.

'Yes, yes! He had it on when he was telling the people that he was getting old and his son was taking his place.'

'I wonder how it came to be lying in the glen – something so precious and important,' wondered Fattie.

'There must be a story behind that,' said Dad. 'A pretty tragic one, I wouldn't wonder.'

'Seamas Dhu will know,' said Iain. 'We must go back and see him.'

'We'll do it tomorrow,' said Dad.

9

The Treasure of the Mac an Dhus

Next day, Iain, his dad and Mr McFatridge went back to the
Sleepy Glen. When they had walked a good way up the track, Iain
played a tune on his magic chanter. The others stayed a distance
away from him, in case Seamas Dhu chose not to appear to them.
Iain had the piece of horn in his hand. He had memorised the
translation of the words on the parchment, so that he wouldn't
have to take it out. To remind himself, he stopped piping and
spoke the words out loud: 'Hidden by water, darkened by sunrise,
defended by the hunter, the treasure of the Mac an Dhu.'

'So you've found it!' Seamas Dhu stood beside him with a
hunting dog at his side.

'Yes,' said Iain. 'Do you know about it?'

'Oh yes, I know.'

'What does it mean?'

'Ah, that you must find out for yourself.'

'Was this the piece of horn that old Domnall Ruraidh wore
round his neck?'

'Indeed it was.'

'How did it come to be lying in the glen?'

'That's a dark story,' said Seamas grimly. 'When he handed over
the lairdship to his son, and he saw what he did to the glen, he
wouldn't part with the horn. He was set upon one night in the
dark and the horn was ripped from the thong. It's not hard to
work out who arranged that. But the thief himself came to grief
– some say he was misled by an *each-uisge*, a kelpie – and he fell off

his pony and was killed. The horn must've fallen with him and was never found. It was often searched for.'

'Do you know what the treasure is?' asked Iain. 'You must tell me. I've got to know, otherwise who's going to believe me?'

Seamas looked at him darkly. 'I'm not compelled to tell you anything,' he said. 'I know what the treasure is all right. But you must find out for yourself.'

'Won't you even give me a clue?' demanded Iain in exasperation.

'Clues? Is it clues you want?'

'Yes, please,' begged Iain, trying not to push too hard.

Seamas stood silent for a moment. 'You've had from me pearls of wisdom,' he said at last, 'pearls beyond price. Watch where my dog goes!' At a signal, the dog by his side streaked away up the glen and up the hillside, through the whins and stones, disappearing and reappearing with the rise and fall of the ground, till he stood high on a crag beside a waterfall.

Seamas went striding off in the same direction, leaving Iain to puzzle over his words. 'Pearls of wisdom. Pearls beyond price. Watch where my dog goes.'

Dad and Fattie came hurrying up the path. 'What did he say?' asked Dad when he got his breath back.

'Did he tell you about the treasure?' Fattie wanted to know.

'No,' said Iain. 'He didn't. He sort of gave me a clue, but I don't understand it.'

'What did he say?'

'Something about pearls of great price. Then he told me to watch where his dog went.'

'And where did his dog go?'

'It ran up the hillside on to a big rock.'

'Which one?'

'That one up there.'

They gazed up at the rock and Iain thought he could see Seamas Dhu and his dog on top of it.

'That's a really big rock,' remarked Fattie. 'I wonder if it's got a name.'

'I don't know,' said Iain. 'They certainly had names for them long ago. There was a story about someone who leapt from Hunter's Rock to the Lover's Crag over the White Linn.'

'Well, there's a waterfall beside that rock and – look! a bit further over and lower down – there's another rock. That could be where the story happened.'

'Yes,' said Iain excitedly, 'so it could. That high one could be Hunter's Rock.'

'Didn't the parchment say something about the hunter?'

'Defended by the hunter,' repeated Iain. 'That could be it. It might be under that rock.'

'Pearls beyond price,' chimed in Dad. 'What do you suppose that meant? How do pearls come into it?'

Iain couldn't think at first, then something else came back into his mind from his time with Seamas Dhu. 'Seamas Dhu had a pearl. He said his father got it in the burn. He said there were lots of them, although it took patience to find them.'

'Freshwater pearls!' exclaimed Fattie. 'Of course! Tayside's famous for them. Remember, there was one on show in Cairncross, the jeweller's, that was worth a fortune.'

'Oh yes,' said Dad, 'I went to look at it. That was found by a local pearl fisher. I think his name was Abernethy. A beautiful stone.'

'Maybe that's what the treasure is,' said Iain.

'Could be.'

'It takes patience to find them,' Fattie reminded them, 'it takes patience to find them, because . . . '

'They're hidden by water!' shouted Iain.

'That could mean the treasure is hidden in all the streams in the glen,' cried Dad in dismay. 'Och, I knew there was bound to be a catch in it! A lot of these old rhymes that sound as if they're about some great mystery are just oblique ways of saying something quite simple. There are pearls to be found in the water, that's all it means.'

'But everyone would know that,' said Iain, 'so why did Domnall Ruraidh have it written on parchment and why did he carry it about in a bit of deer's horn?'

'Maybe he just wanted to create a mystery,' said Dad.

'Who for? Would it be a mystery to the people of the glen?' demanded Iain.

'Oh, I'm not sure,' said Dad. 'I don't know what to think.'

'Darkened by sunrise,' Fattie repeated another of the clues from the parchment. 'I wonder what that can mean. Sunrise usually brings light. How can it darken anything?'

'We'd need to come back at the crack of dawn to see,' said Dad.

'We could camp overnight,' Iain suggested eagerly. 'Oh please, Dad! That'd be double-doss!'

Fattie took something from his pocket and looked at it closely.

'What's that?' asked Iain.

'A compass. See, that's the north,' he pointed ahead. 'Over there is due east. That's where the sun rises.'

'Behind Hunter's Rock,' said Dad. 'That means this side of the rock and even the waterfall would be in shadow at first light.'

'Darkened by sunrise!' shouted Iain, making Bitsy bark joyfully.

'The dog!' said Fattie, becoming more enthusiastic. '"Watch where my dog goes".'

'That's what Seamas Dhu said. And his dog went to the rock!'

'Iain, you and I are going to the top of that rock. Mr Barlass, you hold Bitsy till we get up there. Then let him go and we'll whistle and yell to bring him up to us. We'll watch where he goes.' He turned to Iain. 'Did you see exactly where Seamas Dhu's dog went, all the way up?'

'Well, no,' said Iain. 'I could see him most of the time, but every now and then he'd disappear behind things – bushes or stones – or into a hollow.'

'Right. We'll need to watch Bitsy carefully.'

'It'll take you a bit of time to get up there,' said Dad. 'You'd better take a sandwich with you. And take care!'

They shared out the sandwiches and Iain and Fattie set off for Hunter's Rock. It was quite a long walk and fairly rough going once they left the beaten track and struck up the hillside. It took them almost an hour to reach the base of the rock.

'It's too steep to climb,' said Fattie. 'We'll have to go round it and get on to it from that ridge.'

This again took time and they were both out of breath by the time they stood on the flat rock beside the roaring linn, looking down the glen. They could hardly see Dad and Bitsy, who looked like toy figures in the distance below, dwarfed by the grand scale of the surroundings. The hills were like a circle of giants who seemed to hold them in the hollow of their hands. On a sunny day like this, they looked quite benevolent but Iain could imagine that in a winter blizzard their dark looming shapes could look sinister and hostile. As if reading his thoughts, Fattie said, 'I wouldn't like to be up here in December!'

'Neither would I,' agreed Iain, 'but doesn't it look great today?'

'Better give your Dad a wave to make sure he can see us and so's he'll let Bitsy go. He won't hear us yelling or whistling till he gets a good bit nearer.'

'Bitsy will know what to do. He watched us all the way up here.'

'I'm sure.' Fattie took out a white hankie and waved it above his head. Iain took off his T-shirt and did the same. With an answering wave, Dad let Bitsy go. The dog bounded off towards them and never swerved for an instant except to dodge round boulders and bushes.

'He can fairly move!' said Fattie.

Iain was fizzing with excitement as he watched Bitsy coming up the hillside. 'Bitsy! Bitsy! Come on!' he yelled. As he got nearer, Iain could hear him barking madly.

'Keep your eyes on him when he gets near the rock,' shouted Fattie.

As Bitsy climbed up and up, they had to go almost to the edge of the rock to see him. Then he veered to the right, in the direction of the waterfall, and disappeared into the hillside. Iain ran to the other side and peered over. 'Bitsy!' He almost had to scream to be heard over the sound of the falling water. There came an answering bark that seemed to have a hollow booming echo to it.

'Where is he?' asked Fattie.

'He seems to have gone in somewhere,' replied Iain. The rock was roughly worn into ledges above the linn, and he cautiously stepped down a bit from the top to see if he could catch a glimpse of the dog. 'Bitsy! Bitsy!' he called again and once more came an answering yelp from the bowels of the hill.

'Be careful!' warned Fattie. 'Watch where you put your feet. Hold on tightly and don't lean out too far.'

Iain tried to follow his advice but one of the stones he put his foot on was loose and sent a shower of fragments to be swallowed up in the cascade below. Iain shivered for a minute. This was really dangerous. If he fell, that would be the end of him.

'Come back!' Fattie told him sharply, but when he looked up, he didn't think he could. He was stuck. His mouth dried up and he began to feel dizzy. Fattie leaned over and tried to reach him, but he was too far away. Bitsy was barking endlessly down below, his barks resounding as if he was inside a cave. Iain swallowed hard and tried to steady up. Then the thought of solving the mystery of the treasure made him forget his fear.

'I think there must be a cave under the rock,' he shouted.

'Don't try to get to it,' Fattie told him firmly. 'Just hold on till your Dad comes and we'll get you back up.'

'But . . . ' Iain protested.

'Do as I say. We can come back again with proper equipment and find the cave.'

'But what about Bitsy?' Iain tried to edge down another few feet, but this time his foot slipped and before he knew it, he was falling. 'This is it!' he thought, then he blacked out.

When he came to, he was aware first of the loud roaring noise of the water, then of his father bending over him and Bitsy licking his face.

'Lie still, son,' Dad told him. 'Don't move till we see if you've broken anything.'

'What happened?' asked Iain faintly.

'You fell on to a ledge and Bitsy kept you from rolling off. He held on to your jeans with his teeth, just the way he used to do, to keep you from running across the road and getting knocked down.'

'Good old Bitsy!' chittered Iain. He was cold and wet and felt miserable. 'Where are we?'

'We seem to be behind the linn. It's not really a cave, just an overhang with a shelf under it.' Dad was testing his arms and legs gently. 'Does it hurt anywhere?'

'Not really,' said Iain.

'Can you move your hands and feet?'

Iain wiggled his toes and ankles, his fingers and wrists.

'Good. Try sitting up.' Dad put an arm round him and drew him carefully into a sitting position. 'All right?'

Iain nodded. He felt rather bruised and battered, but seemed to have survived the fall.

'My, you're lucky!' Dad said with relief. He helped Iain to his feet. The waterfall was a wall of blinding light and noise a few feet away. Behind them was solid rock. Bitsy was snuffing about, feeling able to explore now that Iain was on his feet again.

'How did *you* get here?' Iain asked his father.

'More by luck than anything else. When I got up to the rock

and Mr McFatridge said you'd fallen, I just scrambled down any way I could. It's a wonder I didn't fall myself.'

'How are we going to get back?'

'That I don't know,' said Dad, 'but we'll find a way, don't worry.'

Just then Bitsy barked and when they looked round, they couldn't see him. He barked again and the noise seemed to be coming from behind a boulder. It was at the mouth of a hole in the rock, and Bitsy had obviously squeezed inside. It wasn't a very big hole; Iain could just about crawl into it, but Dad couldn't.

'Bitsy!' he shouted, as he scrambled through the rocky opening. 'Where are you?'

The little cave was dark and Iain could see nothing at first. Bitsy was snuffling and growling somewhere near him. Iain crept forward a few yards till he felt a barrier in front of him. He seemed to have reached the limits of the cave. It was little more than a hole in the rock. 'Come on Bitsy,' he whispered, 'let's get out of here!' He crawled out backwards, hauling Bitsy with him. When they got out of the hole, Iain found Bitsy was holding something in his mouth.

'What's this?'

Bitsy ran round and round with the object between his teeth and Iain was reminded of the time he had run off with Lizzie Blackie's bag on the Inch. 'Give me that, Bitsy,' he ordered. Bitsy laid it dutifully at his feet. It *was* a bag, but old and rotten, and as Iain took hold of it, the fibres disintegrated and it spilled its contents on the ground.

'What on earth is that?' asked Dad.

'Bitsy found it,' said Iain, nearly choking with wild delight. 'It's a bag of – PEARLS! It's the treasure!'

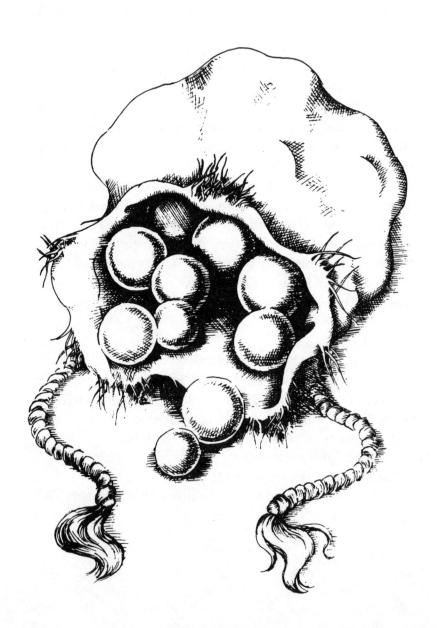

10

Seamas Dhu to the Rescue

They looked at the heap of lustrous stones in utter dumbfounded silence. Each pearl was perfectly round with a silvery blue bloom.

'I've never seen pearls as big as that!' exclaimed Dad. 'They must be worth a fortune!'

'Seamas Dhu's people were pearl fishers,' said Iain. 'They must've been the ones who got them for the Mac an Dhus.'

'It would take centuries to build up a collection like that!'

'I wish Seamas Dhu was here,' said Iain. His chanter was in the rucksack that he'd been carrying when he fell. He felt inside it and brought the chanter out in two pieces. It was shattered – and so was he! 'The magic chanter!' he wailed. 'It's broken!'

'Oh, you'll be able to get it mended,' said his father.

'I'll take it to Geordie Blackie,' said Iain.

'No need for that,' said a voice at their back. Turning, they found Seamas Dhu standing there.

'Seamas!' cried Iain in delight. 'Can you mend it?'

Seamas Dhu took the pieces in his hand. 'It was broken in your time,' he said. 'It wasn't broken in mine.'

'Does that mean when you go back the chanter will have been mended?'

'It won't have been broken,' said Seamas. 'So – you've found the treasure of the Mac an Dhus?'

'Yes,' said Iain. 'It looks like it.'

They gathered up the shimmering pearls, counting them as

they did so – there were four hundred of them! They put them in the plastic bag the sandwiches had been in and stowed them carefully into Mr Barlass's stronger rucksack. As they were doing this, there came a faint 'Hallo!' from beyond the curtain of water. It was Fattie.

'Are you okay?' he shouted.

'Hallo!' Dad responded. 'Yes, everything's all right!'

'How do we get out of here?' asked Iain.

'Follow me,' said Seamas Dhu. He led them along the shelf behind the tumbling water, away from Hunter's Rock, and just when Iain thought he couldn't possibly go any farther, they turned a corner and found a narrow shaft in the rock, sloping upwards to the daylight. Seamas Dhu seemed to have no trouble squeezing up through it, and Bitsy scrambled up after him, but Iain couldn't get a foothold.

Seamas leaned down and held his arms out. 'Come on,' he urged. 'I'll pull you up.'

Dad hoisted him part of the way up the chimney till he could grasp Seamas's strong hands and in no time he was out. He found himself on the smaller crag. He waved across to Fattie who was still on Hunter's Rock. Dad emerged from the rocky cleft with a sigh of relief.

'Seamas,' said Iain, 'remember that story about Aonghais Mac an Dhu's ancestor?'

'Which one?' asked Seamas. 'There are many ancestors and many stories.'

'The one who jumped across the White Linn from Hunter's Rock to the Lovers' Crag.'

'Oh, that one.'

'Was it here? Is this it?'

'Yes,' said Seamas Dhu. 'It is.'

They stared at the wide gap between the rocks which looked impossible to jump. 'That's an incredible leap!' said Dad. 'At least fourteen feet, I'd say.'

'When you're running for your life,' said Seamas Dhu, 'all things are possible.'

'Was he?' asked Iain.

'He was that,' replied Seamas. 'At his back was a horde of wild caterans led by Iain an Crupach, Iain the Hunchback of the Clan Donnachaidh. If they'd caught him, he wouldn't have lived to tell the tale.'

'But he did!' cried Iain.

'Yes, he did,' smiled Seamas Dhu, 'and so did you. You could've been killed, *mo ghille beag*, falling down the side of the rock. Lucky your dog saved you. In country like this, you should always have a dog with you.'

'Bitsy's great,' said Iain. 'He can do anything.' He clapped Bitsy's shaggy coat gratefully.

'Hey!' shouted Fattie. 'How do I get over there?'

'You could jump!' yelled Dad. They all laughed.

'I'm not Aonghais Mac an Dhu!'

'You'll need to go down the way you came up,' said Seamas Dhu. 'We'll join you further down the hill.'

They all set off from the two rocks, along the ridges of the hill behind them, then turned off down the hillside, towards the floor of the glen. When they reached more level ground, Seamas Dhu collected some twigs and brushwood and lit a fire in a sheltered hollow. 'You'd better dry those wet clothes,' he said.

Iain and his dad took off their damp things and hung them near the blaze. Seamas gave each of them a plaid to wrap round them meantime. He then produced a tin pan which he filled at the nearby burn and hung above the fire from one end of a stick with the other end stuck into the ground. From a small tin box, he measured out four scoops of tea into the pan with a horn spoon. Dad rummaged in his rucksack and found a few more rolls and a packet of biscuits. Seamas Dhu beamed at them and drew out from under his plaid two dead rabbits. They watched in fascination as he took a knife and skinned and gutted them with incredible speed. Then he held them close to the reddest part of the fire on the point of his dirk.

'I can see why you were so useful when people lived here,' said Fattie.

'Gather up more sticks,' said Seamas Dhu to Iain, 'and keep the fire going.'

They waited for the tea to boil and the rabbits to roast, munching the rolls and biscuits because they were very hungry. When the tea was ready they drank it out of some plastic cups Fattie fished out of his rucksack. Seamas Dhu deftly dismembered the rabbits and shared them out. Iain thought he'd never tasted anything so delicious.

'Well,' said Seamas Dhu, when they'd all finished licking their fingers, 'now that you've found the treasure of the Mac an Dhus, what are you going to do with it?'

'The question is,' said Dad, 'what can we do? How can we explain to people the way we got these pearls?'

'Just tell them the truth,' said Seamas Dhu. 'Your dog found them.'

'They'll think that's a bit strange.'

'Truth is stranger than fiction,' put in Fattie. 'They must be worth thousands of pounds. The question is, who do they belong to?'

'Finders, keepers,' said Iain.

'It's not as simple as that,' said Fattie. 'We'll have to get advice from a lawyer.'

'I tell you what *I* think,' said Dad. 'You showed us a vision of the future, Seamas Dhu. I want to make that vision come true, and I think the pearls will help us to do that.'

Seamas Dhu laughed delightedly and slapped his knee. 'That's right! That's what's meant to happen!'

'Are there any members of the chief of the Mac an Dhu's family still alive? Did Domnall Ruraidh not have any descendants?'

Seamas Dhu smiled grimly. 'Not a soul. The curse of Mairi Mor saw to that. The tinsmiths – my descendants – changed their name to Blackie to avoid the curse.'

'Where did the pearls come from?' asked Iain. 'Did your people find them?'

'Yes,' said Seamas proudly. 'All these pearls were taken from the burns in the glen by my ancestors. They would give the best of their haul to the chief of the Mac an Dhus.'

'Then they really belong to you if they belong to anybody,' said Iain.

'Well, maybe,' said Seamas, 'but I want you to use them to bring life back to the glen, to waken up *Gleann a' Chadail*.'

'We'll do that,' promised Mr Barlass.

'I believe you will,' said Seamas Dhu. He held out his hand to each of them in turn, as if they were sealing a bargain. The fire was still burning in the cool dusk and Iain felt very contented, sitting on the ground, leaning against a mossy stone. Softly Seamas Dhu began to sing:

Gleann a' Chadail, Gleann a' Chadail,
Dear are you in my heart's keeping,
Long, too long, has been your sleeping.

'Why don't you tell us a story?' suggested Iain when the song was over. Dad and Fattie seemed to be under the same spell of peace and tranquility, as they lay stretched out by the fire.

'Well, here's a wee story,' Seamas began.

'Not in my time, nor in your time, but in somebody's time, there was a king who had three sons. The two older sons were kind of sensible boys and did the things princes are supposed to do, but the third one was a bit silly and spent all his time fetching water for the cook in the kitchen. His brothers laughed at him and called him Silly Jack the Water-carrier.

'When the king was getting old, he sent for his sons and said,

"Now, I have to decide who's to be king after me. To do that, I'm going to give you three tasks. Whoever does them best will win the kingdom."

'He took them to the top of the highest tower in the castle and gave them each a feather. "Your first task," he said, "is to see who can find the most beautiful ring. Now, throw your feathers up in the air. Whichever way the wind blows your feather, that's the way you've to go to find your ring."

'They threw the feathers up and one went north and one went south, while Jack's went straight down behind the castle. The two brothers laughed and took to their horses. "Whoever wins, it won't be Silly Jack!"

'They'd a certain time to find the rings and when the time was nearly up, Jack thought he'd take a look behind the castle, just in case his feather was still there. To his surprise, he found it lying beside a big stone with an iron ring in it. On the stone sat a frog, who spoke to Jack. "Hallo, Jack," it said, "you've been a long time coming."

'Jack was amazed to be spoken to by a frog. Then the frog told him to take hold of the iron ring and lift up the stone. Jack heaved and hauled until it shifted and revealed steps leading down below the ground. The frog led him down to a place that was full of frogs having a ceilidh, with pipes and fiddles and lots of good food and drink. Jack had a good time with them and then the frog who had brought him there said, "Now, there's something I have to give you before you go. You've to find a ring, haven't you?"

'"Oh yes," said Jack, "but that's something I couldn't do. Where am I going to get a ring?"

'The frog handed him a wee box and told him to take it back to his father, then bid Jack goodbye.

'Next day, when they were supposed to be back at the castle with their rings, Jack's brothers appeared with two of the most marvellous rings you've ever seen. "These are fine," said the king, "but what has Jack got?"

'While his brothers laughed loudly, Jack took out from his pocket the tiny box the frog had given him and opened it. They were nearly blinded by the brilliance of the ring that was inside.

'"Oh, Jack's ring is definitely the best!" said the king.

'The other princes were dumbfounded, but there was nothing they could do. "I wonder where he stole that?" one said spitefully.

'Next day, the king had them up to the top of the castle again with their feathers. This time, they were to bring back a beautiful table cover. When they threw their feathers up, one went east, one went west, and Jack's went down behind the castle.

'Off went the princes on horseback, while Jack went back down to the kitchen to sit at the fire. "Where am I going to get a table cover?" he wondered. "I'm definitely out of the game this time." Later, he strolled round to the place where the stone with the ring was. The frog was waiting for him.

'"You've come sooner this time, Jack," it said. "You're learning!"

'Down they went again to the place where all the frogs were singing and dancing and playing melodeons. Jack had a lot of fun there with his hospitable friends. Again, before he left, the frog gave him a small parcel. "This is your table cover," it told Jack.

'When the day came that they were to show the king their table covers, Jack's brothers arrived with really wonderful covers of silk and lace, sewn with precious stones, embroidered and fringed with silver and gold. The king was very impressed. But when Jack opened up his parcel, there came out of it a cover the like of which none of them had ever seen.

'"Jack has won again!" said the king. The two brothers were furious!

'Then came the last task, and this was to bring back a beautiful bride. They threw the feathers up and once again one went one way, one went the other, and Jack's went behind the castle. The two princes rode off gleefully; this time they felt sure Jack couldn't possibly win. "What princess would look at him?" they scoffed.

'Jack felt just the same. "Where would I get a girl to marry me?" He was sure the frogs couldn't help him this time. But, all the same, he went for a walk behind the castle and sure enough, the frog was expecting him.

'"Come on down, Jack," it said. "Now you know where to come!"

'Once again, they went down the steps to the ceilidh place. Jack danced all the time with a wee girl frog, who smiled up at him sweetly. When he was about to leave, the big frog said, "Well, Jack, take her with you. She's your bride!"

'"A frog!" cried Jack. "I can't marry a frog! My brothers are really going to get a laugh at me this time."

'"Just take her with you," said the big frog.

'Well, Jack and the wee girl frog went up the steps and as soon as they reached the top, the frog turned into the most beautiful princess that Jack had ever seen. He was almost afraid to look at her. She smiled and took his hand and together they walked round to the front of the castle. There, Jack's father, the king, was standing with his two brothers and their lovely brides. They were both outstandingly pretty, but when you compared them with Jack's princess, they looked plain, even ugly. The two brothers quickly took them away and bundled them into cupboards.

'"That settles it," said the king. "Jack has won the kingdom!"

'And Jack was a good king and ruled for many years. I went round the back of their castle myself and saw them both. They gave me supper off a wee tin table. The table bended and my story's ended.'

'That was great!' said Iain.

Then Fattie asked, 'Isn't it true that these stories always have a meaning?'

'Oh yes,' said Seamas Dhu. 'You can learn wisdom from them. They were our education, you know.'

'What can you learn from that one?' asked Iain. 'It's a good story, but – well, does it mean that the silliest person always wins?'

'Not quite,' said Seamas Dhu. 'You have to think about it.'

'We'll have to be getting home,' said Dad, stretching. 'We've quite a way to walk back to the car.'

'Well,' said Seamas Dhu, 'I must take my leave of you, too. We'll not be meeting again.'

'Oh,' said Iain in dismay. 'But why?'

'It's the end of the story,' said Seamas Dhu. 'The happy ending, I hope. *Gleann a' Chadail* will awaken now.'

He stood up and drew his plaid around him. The fire was dying out and the sunset was fading in the sky. 'Goodbye,' he said, and strode off into the darkening glen.

The three of them watched till Seamas Dhu had disappeared, then they walked back down the glen to where the car was parked. Iain thought about Seamas's story about the feathers. 'I bet Geordie and Lizzie know it and could tell me what it means,' he thought to himself. 'I'll ask them next time I see them.'

11

Comings and Goings

A great many things began to happen after the discovery of the treasure. When Iain got home with Dad and Fattie, they showed the pearls to Mum, who nearly fainted when she saw their blue light glimmering on her dining table.

'What are we going to do with them?' she wanted to know.

'I'll have to find out what the law says,' replied Dad. 'They'll have to be put in a safe place, like a bank vault.'

'We're going to bring the glen back to life,' said Iain. 'We're going to do things like Seamas Dhu has shown us.'

'That'll be some task,' said Fattie. 'We'll need a lot of help and organisation.'

They talked till it was quite late, then the pearls were put away, this time in a velvet bag Mum had looked out.

'Time for bed, Iain,' she said. 'You've had a long day.'

'It's been a great day, double-doss great. But I'm not really tired,' Iain assured her, then yawned before he could stop himself. 'Bitsy's a hero dog!'

When he went to bed, he was so tired he couldn't sleep for a long time. His head was full of all kinds of thoughts and pictures that kept repeating and repeating themselves. Most of all, he kept reliving the episode behind the linn, when Bitsy found the treasure. When he did fall asleep, his dreams were full of the shimmer of pearls and he saw the glen with a waterfall of pearls streaming down it and Seamas Dhu standing on Hunter's Rock, playing his pipes in triumph.

Next day, Dad was up early. 'Now, Iain,' he said over breakfast, 'we have to do things according to the law. I'm asking the police to send someone round. We'll have to give the pearls into their keeping to start with.'

'But if you tell them what we promised Seamas Dhu, they'll let us keep them, won't they?' cried Iain in alarm.

'Now, Iain, listen to me! We can't start telling the police stories about phantom pipers and magic chanters and visits to the past. They won't believe us. They may think we're trying to cover up a crime.'

Iain was aghast. 'But we've got to tell them the truth, Dad! We can't tell lies!'

'We aren't going to tell any lies,' said Dad. 'We'll tell them how Bitsy found the bag of pearls. We can tell them that exactly as it happened.'

'But they'll wonder what we were doing and why we were behind the waterfall.'

'Well, there again, we can tell the truth. We were on a day's outing. You and Mr McFatridge climbed up to the rock. Then Bitsy followed you and got behind the linn. You were trying to get to him when you fell and I came up and found you. Then Bitsy discovered the pearls. That is what happened.'

'Yes, but . . . ' Iain felt it sounded so ordinary. He wanted the whole fantastic story to be known.

'Don't worry, son. It'll all work out in the end. Now, the Procurator Fiscal has to decide who the pearls belong to.'

'Who's he?' asked Iain.

'He's a Court official who has to decide legal questions.'

'But we *know* who the pearls belong to,' Iain protested. 'We can tell him.'

'Look,' said Dad, 'we can't tell him that, not without going into all the story of the glen and Seamas Dhu. We can't do that.'

Just then, the doorbell rang and Mum brought Mr McFatridge in.

'I've just been explaining to Iain about the Procurator Fiscal,' said Dad.

'What if he says we can't have the pearls?' asked Iain. 'How can you explain what you want to use them for without telling him about Seamas Dhu?'

'I'll find a way,' Dad promised.

'You could point out that the pearls belong to the glen,' suggested Fattie. 'They're a resource, like coal or oil.'

'Yes,' said Dad. 'It's not as if we want the pearls or the money they're worth for ourselves. We'll ask to be allowed to set up a public trust fund to develop the glen.'

'What's that?' asked Iain.

'It means we'll sign papers that say the money will be used only for that purpose and nothing else.'

There was another ring at the doorbell and this time it was Inspector Davidson from the County Police Headquarters; a tall thin man in an extremely smart uniform. He was stunned when Mr Barlass opened the velvet bag and poured out the treasure on to the table.

'This is treasure trove with a vengeance,' he said in a hushed voice, whose very quietness seemed to underline his astonishment. He asked a lot of questions and took a lot of notes till Iain began to get restless. Dad had said pointedly to him that he should just answer any questions the Inspector asked, implying that he should otherwise hold his tongue, and it wasn't an easy thing to do with such a story as he had bottled up inside him.

At last the Inspector seemed to have got all the information he wanted. 'The stones would normally be sent to the Procurator Fiscal,' he said. 'However, considering the immense value of the hoard, I think they'd better be put immediately into safekeeping in a vault somewhere, possibly a bank. I'll arrange that. I'll be in touch by phone within the hour and a security van will come and take them away. You'll get a receipt. I'll also inform the Procurator Fiscal and you'll then hear from him.'

The Inspector took his leave and Iain suddenly felt really deflated and empty. All the magic, all the visions, all the extraordinary experiences he'd had seemed to have vanished. Everything had been taken over by the matter-of-factness of the grown-up world. He crept up to his room and left his dad and his teacher talking in the living-room. With his arm round Bitsy, he sighed deeply and wondered, with all the legal business that was beginning to seem so complicated, whether the treasure would ever be used as they wanted.

'Why do grown-ups have to make everything so difficult?' he muttered to Bitsy.

When he went downstairs again, Fattie had gone and Dad was sitting at his desk writing busily.

'What are you doing, Dad?' asked Iain.

'I'm setting out my ideas to satisfy the Procurator Fiscal that I'm not planning to sell the pearls and emigrate.'

'Maybe that's what you should do,' said Iain, gloomily. 'It'd be a lot easier!'

'Oh, yes!' said Dad ironically. 'That'd be very easy! And it'd be just as easy to catch us and clap us in jail!'

'But why should they do that?'

'Because the pearls are now Crown property, not ours.'

'Does that mean the Queen owns them?'

'I suppose so.'

'That's not fair!' declared Iain decisively. 'She's got enough of her own!'

Dad laughed. 'It doesn't mean they're her personal property. They're just under royal protection till it's decided what's to happen to them.'

Iain sighed. 'What a fuss!' he said. 'It's been decided already, anyway.'

'Don't worry,' said Dad again. 'I know you don't understand the reason for all this, but it's for the best.'

Next day, Dad had to go and see the Procurator Fiscal, Mr

Menzies. Iain begged to be allowed to go with him and, in the end, Dad agreed.

The office was in Tay Street, overlooking the Queen's Bridge. Mr Menzies was a slightly built, quiet-spoken elderly man, with a smooth leathery face, who welcomed them very pleasantly.

'Now, Mr Barlass,' he said in a buttery voice when they had shaken hands and seated themselves in front of his large desk. 'There is a decision to be made about these pearls. They are, I understand, of considerable value – very considerable value! I thought I should like to speak to you first. And this is the young man who found them?'

'Yes, sir,' said Iain.

'Good, good. Now, you know that, by law, they belong to the Crown.'

'Yes,' said Dad. 'But if you'll be good enough to read this document I've prepared, perhaps you'll consider the suggestions it contains and advise me of their feasibility.'

'It's all going to be long words and complicated phrases,' moaned Iain silently, wondering what would happen if he told this solemn-faced gnome of the law the secrets behind the finding of the treasure. He wriggled in his seat and Dad gave him a warning glance.

Mr Menzies put on his reading glasses and carefully read the paper Dad had handed to him. He read it and re-read it several times impassively then took off his glasses.

'Thank you, Mr Barlass,' he said. 'This has certainly added a new dimension to this affair. I shall have to consult the Queen's and Lord Treasurer's Remembrancer in Edinburgh to see if the Crown will countenance your proposals. You want to set up a public trust fund to rehabilitate the glen. Well, as Procurator Fiscal, I have no objections to that. It seems an honest and commendable intention. It may be that the Crown will also approve, subject to certain conditions.' Iain's heart began to beat faster at his words. This sounded more promising!

'What conditions?' asked Dad.

'Well, they might want some of the pearls to be put on exhibition in the National Museum, or even in Perth Museum.'

'We'd agree to that, I think,' said Dad.

'I'll get in touch with the Remembrancer right away,' said Mr Menzies, 'but it may be some time before I have an answer. There is, I believe, a committee which will have to consider the idea.'

'Of course,' said Dad. 'Thank you very much.'

Mr Menzies smiled at them. 'Good luck,' he said, and held out his hand. They shook hands and took their leave.

As they walked home, Iain said, 'He was quite a nice man. I don't think he'll make us give up the pearls.'

'He was very nice indeed,' agreed Dad. 'He can't do anything off his own bat, but I think he's on our side.'

'What sort of things did you suggest, Dad? You know, for the glen?'

'Well, I haven't talked to anyone about them, but I mentioned things like water projects of some kind – the glen's got very pure water – and things to do with game and fish, there's plenty of those. There could be scientific things as well.'

'There's millions of things!' Iain agreed. 'The glen could be a busy place again.'

Nothing much happened after that and in a few days the school term began again, which gave Iain the chance to tell Neil about his adventures and finding the treasure. As usual, Neil was hard to convince, especially about the treasure. 'Just wait,' Iain told him, 'and you'll see it's true.'

One Saturday after lunch, Iain decided to take his new bike and cycle out to see Geordie and Lizzie at Birkenhaugh. He knew Dad would have taken him, if he'd asked, because they had spoken about it. But Iain wanted to talk to them by himself. It was quite a long way to the caravan site, but at last he reached it and made his way to Geordie and Lizzie's trailer. They gave him a tremendous welcome.

'Come in!' roared Geordie. 'Here's the man himsel!'

'Sit ye doon, son,' said Lizzie, drawing him into their midst.

'Have ye a story tae tell, eh?' Geordie asked with a wink.

'Oh yes!' Iain assured him. It was great to be away from all the talk of the law and the Crown, and back to the magic and excitement of the world of Seamas Dhu.

'Let's hear aa aboot it, then!' Geordie demanded.

Iain told them how they found the bit of parchment with the clues on it and how they had worked out where the treasure was. He described how Seamas had helped to lead them to it and how the treasure was found, how Bitsy had gone behind the linn and how he had fallen trying to rescue his dog. They cheered and gasped and crowed as the story unfolded, patting him on the head and shoulders and slapping his back with delight.

'Ye micht hae been mowdit!' cried Lizzie, when he talked of his fall.

'What's that? Mowdit?'

'Lizzie's saying ye micht hae been killt,' Geordie explained. 'Ye micht hae been deid!'

'Is that a traveller's word?' asked Iain.

'Naw, naw,' replied Geordie, 'that's just a Scots word, but ye'll only hear it fae some o the auld folk noo. But tell me whit's happened wi the treasure?'

Iain tried to explain about the Police Inspector and the Procurator Fiscal, but Lizzie's and Geordie's faces grew longer and longer and they fell silent.

'What's the matter?' he asked, although he thought he knew what they were going to say. For a few minutes they said nothing, but gazed glumly at the floor. Then Lizzie gave him a long troubled look.

'Ye'll need tae excuse us, son,' she said, 'but, ye see, that's no oor wey o doin. We like tae keep weel clear o the polis.'

'So does everybody,' said Iain, 'but Dad says this is the right thing to do and it'll all work out in the end.'

'Aye, mebbe,' said Geordie, then he took up a chanter that was lying beside him and started to play a tune. Iain couldn't believe his eyes. It was the magic chanter!

'Where did you get that?'

Geordie stopped playing. 'I tellt ye afore, son. It wis ma grandfaither's grandfaither's.'

'That was Seamas Dhu,' said Iain. 'He took my chanter back to his time, before it got broken. How did you get it?'

'I got it frae ma faither,' smiled Geordie.

'But you gave it to me and I broke it and Seamas Dhu . . . '

'Dinnae ask sae mony questions, baby,' advised Lizzie. 'Hae a wee cup o tea.'

Iain took the cup and was soon munching reflectively through a ham roll. Lizzie was right. He shouldn't question the reappearance of the chanter too much. It was part of the same magic that made it possible for him to meet Seamas Dhu and see the Sleepy Glen in the past. Thinking of Seamas Dhu, he was reminded of the story of the feathers.

'Do you know a story about a king who made his sons do three tasks?' he asked Geordie.

'Aye, aye.'

'They had to throw feathers up in the air.'

'Oh, that yin. That's "The Three Feathers",' replied Geordie. 'Mony's a time I hae tellt it tae ma bairns.'

'What does it mean?'

'Mean?' Geordie was bemused. 'It doesnae mean nuthin. It's a story.'

'Why did Silly Jack win, then?' Iain tried again. 'Why was he the one that got the kingdom?'

'That's easy,' said Geordie. 'He wasnae silly at aa. He was really the maist sensible yin. Ye see, he fund he didnae need tae gang tae the ends o the earth for whit he needed. It was aa richt there aside him, if he jist looked.'

'I see,' said Iain a bit doubtfully.

'That's true,' continued Geordie. 'It's whit I've aye fund tae be true. Dinna think ye need tae sail the seiven seas, nor traivel in foreign lands. Jist look aboot ye an ye'll aye find a livin.'

'Well,' said Iain, 'some people might agree with you. Some people wouldn't. People are different.'

'Aye, aye,' said Geordie. 'Aabody's different. I ken that fine. An I dinna mind people bein different fae me. But there's an affa lot o people wha mind me bein different fae them.'

'What do you mean?' said Iain.

'Och, that's anither story. Yin thing's sure. Ye're no een o them.'

'Naw, naw,' agreed Lizzie. 'Ye're a rare wee lad, so ye are.'

The trailer door opened and Gravy came in looking hot and tired, but when he saw Iain, he gave a great shout of welcome.

'Iain! It's yersel! Hoo are ye, wee man?'

'Fine,' said Iain.

Lizzie bustled about getting tea for Gravy while Geordie played another tune on the chanter.

'Geordie,' said Iain, 'do you remember you said you'd teach me to play the pipes?'

Geordie broke off in the middle of his tune and looked hard at Iain. 'Aye, I mind that. Ye'll hae tae start wi the chanter, ye ken.'

'Yes,' said Iain, 'I know, but I haven't got one now.'

'Here,' said Geordie, rummaging beneath his seat and bringing out another one, 'tak this and I'll show ye hoo tae begin.'

Iain took it and tried to blow a note through it, but once again experienced the feeling he'd had when he first tried the magic chanter.

'Naw,' said Geordie, 'nae like that,' and he showed Iain how to position his mouth properly. Gravy fell asleep after he'd drunk his tea and Lizzie disappeared into the other part of the trailer to attend to some chores. The time sped by unheeded as Iain got his first piping lesson until he suddenly noticed it was half past seven, long past dinner time at home.

'Oh!' he cried in dismay. 'I'll need to get back. They'll wonder where I've got to.'

Gravy stirred and opened his eyes. 'Dinna fash, son. I'll drive ye back intae the toon.'

'But I've got my bike.'

'Pit it on the roof, son.'

'Och, but you're tired,' said Iain. 'It's not fair having to give me a lift.'

'I'm no haein tae gie ye a lift,' retorted Gravy, rising. 'I'm goin intae the toon tae meet ma cousin at the ten-pin bowlin.'

'Oh well,' said Iain, 'that's not so bad.'

'Come back, wee man, ony time,' said Geordie. 'Ony time.'

'I will,' promised Iain.

'Tell us whit happens tae the treisure,' begged Lizzie.

'I will,' promised Iain again.

'Richt! We're for the road,' said Gravy, so they went out and he fastened Iain's bike to the roof-rack of his car. Geordie and Lizzie waved them off and it didn't take long to get back to Iain's house.

Iain half expected his mum to be on the doorstep anxiously waiting for him, but as they drew near the house, it seemed that there was something else going on. A cluster of people, some with cameras, stood on the path.

'Ye seem tae hae some visitors,' said Gravy with a laugh.

'I don't know who they are,' said Iain.

'Press,' said Gravy. 'The newspapers.' He got out of the car and took Iain's bike down from the roof. 'If I was ye, I'd gang in the back door, son.'

'Right,' said Iain, 'I will. Thank you for the lift.'

Gravy got back in the car and waved as he drove off. 'I'll see ye when I see ye!'

Iain wheeled his bike quickly round the back lane and into the back garden. He put it in the shed and went in the back door as quietly as he could. A hubbub of noise greeted him in the house.

He found Mum and Dad in the sitting-room with a whole lot of people he'd never seen before. When he came in, his mother rushed forward and grabbed him.

'Where have you been?' she demanded in an angry voice, pulling him outside.

'I went to see Geordie and Lizzie and I stayed too long. I'm sorry, Mum.'

'Geordie and Lizzie who?'

'They're descendants of Seamas Dhu. Remember, you met him in the glen?'

'Geordie and Lizzie *who*?' insisted his mother.

'Blackie,' said Iain. 'You know old Lizzie.'

'The old woman who collects the rags?'

'Seamas Dhu was Geordie's grandfather's grandfather,' Iain told her.

'But where do they live?'

'Out at Birkenhaugh. They've got a smashing trailer there.'

'Did you go there?'

'Of course. I've been twice now. Geordie gave me the magic chanter. He says I can go back anytime.'

'I don't know about that,' said Mum. 'That's a dangerous place.'

'Who told you that?' Iain demanded. 'You wouldn't say that if you'd been there. It's just like a wee village.'

'But they say some of these travellers . . . '

'They say? Who say?' Iain was echoing something he had heard his mum say many a time. 'You shouldn't pay attention to what "they" say. You should judge for yourself. Isn't that what you always say?'

'Yes,' agreed his mother a bit reluctantly. She had always heard it said in the town that you couldn't trust travelling people, yet she couldn't really say she'd ever had any evidence to support this. It was just prejudice, she reflected. Iain was right – she had always taught him to judge people as he found them and she must do the same.

'They've been very good to me,' Iain assured her. 'They always made sure I got home safely. Gravy brought me back.'

'Who's Gravy?'

'His real name's Graham. He's Geordie's and Lizzie's son. One of their sons.'

'Does your Dad know you've visited them?'

'Yes, he does,' said Iain impatiently. 'Mum, who are all these people?'

'I think the whole of Perth's here,' she said. 'There's people from the council, business people, our lawyer, our bank manager, reporters – I don't know who isn't here.'

More people seemed to be coming in all the time.

'Mum, I'm starving,' said Iain. 'I had something to eat at Geordie's and Lizzie's, but that was a while ago.'

'I kept your dinner warm,' said Mum. 'Come on into the kitchen and I'll get it for you. You'll have to eat it there.'

As Iain wolfed down his mince and tatties, his mother told him how they'd just got word during the day that it was going to be possible to use the treasure to set up a public trust fund for the glen. 'It's a bit more complicated than that, of course,' she said.

'Of course,' said Iain with a sigh. 'Surprise, surprise!'

'But there doesn't appear to be any big problems and there seems to be plenty of people interested already.'

'Great!' said Iain.

'It's not official yet. There's a lot of rigmarole to go through with the law. Maybe your Dad can explain it better than me. But it'll work out.'

'If it's not official,' said Iain, 'why are the reporters here?'

'Well, we can't tell them much,' said Mum. 'We can only really tell them that the treasure was found.'

'Will it be in the papers?'

'Of course.'

Iain grinned. Neil would have to believe him now! When he'd finished his apple pie he asked, 'Can I go and speak to Dad?'

'Well, he's rather busy talking to people, but on you go.'

Iain went into the sitting-room and squeezed through the crowd of people to where his dad was standing near the window.

'Hallo, Dad,' he said.

His father turned. 'Ah now, here's the hero of the story,' he told the people round him. 'This is Iain who found the treasure.'

'Well, really it was my dog, Bitsy,' he began. He couldn't see Bitsy anywhere. Like all sensible animals, he was keeping well out of the way of all the fuss. Cameras clicked and flashed round Iain and a man with a notebook started firing questions at him. 'How old are you? Do you often go hill-walking? What class are you in at school? How far did you walk?' He was soon joined by several others, who asked even sillier questions. 'Do you like rock music? What's your favourite television programme? Do you think boys should wear ear-rings?'

Iain's head was going round with all the noise in the room and everyone talking to him at once. He couldn't answer any of the questions because he couldn't get a word in edgeways or any other way. He was glad when Fattie came and put an arm round his shoulder and drew him out into the hall, saying to the reporters, 'I think that'll do. He's had enough for now.'

One by one, the reporters left, then Dad shook hands with everyone else and they all went away, including Fattie. 'Remember the meeting on Tuesday,' Mr Barlass called after him.

'What a crowd!' Iain said.

'It kind of snowballed,' said Dad. 'It began with word from Edinburgh and a phone call from Mr Menzies. Then I got Mr Pitcaithly, my lawyer, to come round. After that we got in touch with business people and some of them were so interested, they came, including the President of the Chamber of Commerce. Then some of the District Council and after that I lost count.'

'Who told the papers?'

'I don't really know. It wasn't my idea. Someone must've phoned them. We could've done without that; it's much too early to put anything in the papers, apart from the finding of the treasure.'

'But the glen will come back to life?'

'If only it was as easy as that!' Dad laughed. 'But the pearls are worth a lot of money. Someone from Cairncross's has inspected them. They're all much bigger than the freshwater pearls you get nowadays. He wasn't too keen to put a figure on them, but I persuaded him to give me a rough estimate.'

'How much?' breathed Iain.

'Now, if I tell you, you mustn't tell anyone else – yet! Promise?'

'I promise,' said Iain.

'Upwards of fifty thousand pounds.'

Iain whistled. 'Double-doss! A hundred doss!'

'Well, it sounds like a lot of money, but it won't go very far nowadays towards rebuilding a community. No, you see, that's where the business people will come in. They like the idea, so if they're also willing to put money in, we may get somewhere. The Council will help as well.'

'It's going to take ages!' Iain sighed.

'Well, Rome wasn't built in a day. We haven't got magic powers like Seamas Dhu. But at least we've started.'

'I suppose so,' said Iain.

'Time for bed now,' said Dad. 'By the way, where did you get to this afternoon?'

'I was out seeing Geordie and Lizzie Blackie. I don't think Mum's too pleased. She thinks it's too dangerous for me to go there.'

'Don't worry, son, I'll talk to her.'

'It's not like she thinks. They're really good to me and take care of me. Geordie's teaching me to play the pipes.'

'Did you tell them about the treasure?'

'Of course. They were delighted. But they always said it was meant to happen. They're not sure about it going to the police, though.'

Mr Barlass chuckled. 'I'm sure they're not. But they needn't worry. No one's broken the law.'

'Dad,' begged Iain, 'once we know what's to happen, will you come with me and tell Geordie and Lizzie about it?'

'Of course I will. Whatever happens, they must be involved too. They're the last of the Mac an Dhus and the treasure is their treasure.'

Iain went upstairs and told Bitsy all about the events of the day. 'I'm sorry I couldn't take you to Birkenhaugh, but I went on my bike.' Bitsy licked his face as if to say, 'That's all right.' Then Iain got into bed and fell into a dreamless sleep.

12

A Dream Come True

Next day, Iain's photograph was not only in the local papers but the national dailies as well, under headlines like, 'Tayside Treasure Trove' and 'Perth Boy's Pearl Harvest'. His classmates were amazed. Some were delighted and felt they shared in the fame he'd brought. Others, of course, were envious and tried to belittle the importance of it all.

'You found some pearls – so what? Do you think that makes you somebody?'

'No,' said Iain. 'I don't matter at all. It's what we can do with the money.'

'Oh yes?' they sneered. 'Is Daddy going to buy you a computer or a Rolls Royce?'

'No.' Iain tried to explain, 'We're going to use it to bring people back to live in that glen we visited.'

They could make nothing of this, so they made do with some derisive laughter which Iain ignored.

He was certainly right in thinking it would take ages to get things moving. His father had to go to endless meetings and people came constantly to the house. The telephone never stopped ringing and, from time to time, reporters called. In spite of Iain's complaints, Dad wouldn't let him get too much involved. Sometimes, they'd call him in to meet someone, but always on the understanding that he didn't start talking about magic chanters or ghosts of the past.

The result of this was that Iain began to go more and more

often to see Geordie and Lizzie. His piping lessons made good progress and, one day, Geordie let him try to hold a full set of pipes. Iain tucked the bag under his arm, while Geordie placed the drones on his shoulder. It felt like trying to hold an octopus. He got his lips to the mouthpiece and held the chanter, the only bit of the whole contraption that felt familiar, and tried to fill the bag with air. He blew and blew till he was seeing stars and he struggled to control the heaving bag and the wayward drones.

'It's like wrestling with a . . . a . . . some kind of animal!' he laughed, failing to find one to compare it to.

'Aye, it's a wild beast, the pipes!' agreed Geordie, trying hard not to laugh too much, for he could see that Iain was trying very hard. 'Noo, jist try and find a way o haudin them that's steady.'

Iain persevered for a few minutes.

'Jist keep blawin steady intae the bag,' Geordie told him. 'Ye've got tae keep daein that.'

Once he'd got into a position that was reasonably comfortable and was blowing at regular intervals, Geordie encouraged him to try the chanter. It was very different from playing the practice chanter. Iain managed a few notes then had to give up.

'Och, I'll never be able to play these!' he lamented.

'Aye ye will, son. Dinna worry – ye've made a start.'

'It's awful hard to keep on,' complained Iain.

'I ken. But ye hae tae keep on. If you dinna play the pipes, the pipes'll play you!'

They both had a good laugh, Iain picturing a set of pipes marching up and down with Geordie's legs sticking up like drones and his stomach squeezed like a pipe bag.

Iain had by then met other members of Geordie's family. His daughters, Annie and Isy, were both married with families and lived elsewhere, but one day they both visited their parents while Iain was there. Annie was tall and dark, like her father, and talked a lot. Isy was small with fairish hair and had a smoker's cough. They both cuddled Iain, to his intense embarrassment, but they chatted to him in a very friendly way and asked him some funny questions, 'Whit's yer girlfriend's name?' and 'Does yer dug catch rabbits?'

Their brother, Geordie, who was always called Deeks, was the eldest and he was big like his father but was a very quiet man. He never said a word but just stood and looked. Geordie said his nickname was a cant word that meant 'looks'. Deeks had his own trailer on the site, where he lived with his wife, Nancy, and their four children. Whenever Iain saw him, he seemed to be working on car engines or television sets, which he repaired and sold.

Gravy was the one that Iain saw most often and he always enjoyed the company of the cheery scrapman. He frequently got a lift on the 'Gravy Train' – the battered old lorry that Gravy drove.

All this time, of course, he was still in Fattie's class at primary school. He talked with his teacher a lot about the treasure. Iain was usually quite down in the dumps or cross and impatient since so little seemed to be happening. Fattie came to the house from time to time, but all Dad said was, 'Things are just about the same. We're waiting for a decision from the Council,' or 'Not much further forward, I'm afraid. These things take time.'

One Saturday, however, Dad said to him at breakfast, 'Would you like to go to the Sleepy Glen today?'

Iain brightened up right away. 'Oh yes!' he cried. 'Is something going to happen at last?'

'Well, you could say that,' said Dad.

'What? What?' Iain was beside himself with curiosity.

'Wait and see.'

He couldn't get Dad to say any more, so after breakfast Iain went to fetch Bitsy and climbed into the car with Mum and Dad and off they went.

'I wish we could let Geordie and Lizzie know,' said Iain.

'Why not phone the site?' said Dad, so they stopped at a phone box and made the call, asking the warden to give Geordie the message, 'The glen is waking up.'

They flew along the Isla Road, through the winding streets of Blairgowrie to Alyth, to the place where the glen road started. To Iain's surprise, as they got out of the car several other cars drew up behind them.

'Who are these people?' asked Iain.

'Some of them are going to be part of the Glen Trust,' said Dad. 'There's Councillor Wilson and Councillor MacGregor and Mr Mowat, the surveyor, and Mr Christie who's in business.'

They began to walk up the glen road. The broom was out in golden banks on every side and everything looked bright. Iain found the conversation was all facts and figures, so he ran ahead and began to look for the places that were familiar to him. As he no longer had the magic chanter, he couldn't summon up Seamas Dhu to keep him company. He looked around the hillsides, bare apart from the clumps of yellow broom, and wondered what the groups of earnestly talking people were really going to do. He ran back to where Dad was listening to Councillor Wilson and Mr Christie.

'So you'll design this factory for me,' Mr Christie was saying. 'A factory that doesn't look like a factory. Something that people will come to see. A factory that's more than a factory. The sooner, the better. There's a growing market for this product, and a growing demand for facilities such as we will provide.'

'What product?' wondered Iain. 'What on earth could the glen produce that would need a factory?'

Councillor Wilson was saying, 'Now that planning permission has gone ahead for the deer farm, we should get the farmer housed as soon as possible, then we can start on his outbuildings and we can bring in the stock.'

Iain was fascinated by the mention of a deer farm. He'd never heard of such a thing before, and he wondered how deer would take to being reared like cattle. 'I suppose if they're fed and looked after and have lots of room to roam about, they won't mind.'

The Councillor and Mr Christie moved away and Iain tugged

at his father's arm. 'Dad, what's going to be made at the factory?'

Dad looked round in surprise. 'Oh, there you are, Iain. I thought you were away up the glen. You've been listening then?'

'Well, just a bit. I'm dying to know what's going on. I didn't think there'd be any factories in the glen.'

'It's not the usual kind of factory. It's a bottling plant.'

'Bottling? Bottling what?'

'Water. The pure spring water that flows everywhere in the glen. It's got minerals in it that are good for people's health. It's really special. Mr Christie is going to bottle it and sell it. He's also going to have a small hydro – a kind of health centre with a swimming pool.'

'Water!' Iain was struck dumb. The idea of people buying bottles of water seemed so absurd, he could hardly believe it. Dad explained that lots of people bought water like that.

'What about the deer farm?'

'There's a well-to-do farmer who breeds bulls in the Carse of Gowrie interested in that. He's going to help his son set up in the glen as a deer farmer. He's already worked on a deer farm in Fife.'

'That's great!' said Iain.

'Oh, there's more,' said Dad. 'There's a group of people who want to restore the mill and get it working again. Then there's someone talking about a fish farm on the lochan. The Education Authority want to make an outdoor centre for schools. There's no end to the ideas.'

Iain was glad to know that at last the dream was beginning to come true. 'Will the pearls pay for all of this?' he asked.

'Some of it,' said Dad, 'but it'd be impossible without money from the other sources as well – the Council and the business people.'

Iain wandered on ahead again, his eyes imagining the deer on the hillside and the growth of the little village around the bottling plant and health centre. It was to be built of pine and local stone, Dad said, just as they had seen in the vision.

'If only Seamas Dhu were there to hear all this good news,' he wished aloud.

His gaze strayed up to Hunter's Rock and he was startled to see, standing on the crown, a kilted figure holding a set of pipes.

'Seamas Dhu!' he yelled and began to run up the glen towards the rock. He heard the distant sound of the pipes as he ran.

As he got nearer to where he would turn off up the hill, he saw that the piper was moving down the hill to meet him. He was still playing his pipes, striding over hummocks and hollows, down the steep rough slope as if it were level ground. So fast did he move that he was well down the hill before Iain got off the road.

The piper came towards him through the scree and broom at the base of the hill, and Iain saw to his astonishment that it was not Seamas Dhu who was approaching him, but Geordie Blackie.

'Geordie!' he gasped. 'I thought it was Seamas Dhu!'

Geordie stopped a few yards from him and roared with laughter as he tucked his pipes under his arm. 'Ma grandfaither's grandfaither!'

'You really *do* look like him! Iain gasped. 'I told you so! Up there on the rock, nobody would have known the difference.'

'And here, it's only me!' chortled Geordie. 'Are ye disappointed?'

'No, no,' Iain protested. 'But how did you get here so fast?'

'Well, I took a near-cut,' said Geordie, 'a thing ye shouldnae do efter dark. But in the daytime, it's okay. Ye took the high road and I took the low road.'

'Oh, Geordie,' cried Iain. 'I've such good news for you. My Dad's here with some people and they're really going to get things going in the glen. There's to be a deer farm and a factory to bottle spring water. There's going to be a health place as well.'

Geordie sat down on a big stone and looked thoughtful. 'A deer fairm,' he repeated. 'And a bottle factory. Weel, weel.'

By this time, Iain's dad and the others were coming up the glen road and were not very far behind them.

Iain ran back and begged his dad to come and meet Geordie.

'I'd be delighted,' said Dad, 'we can all meet Geordie. I've got an idea that I want to put to him.'

When they got back to where Geordie was sitting, he stood up very straight and looked at them calmly.

'This is my Dad,' Iain said. 'Dad, this is my friend, Geordie Blackie.'

The two men shook hands, 'I'm really pleased to met you, Geordie,' said Dad warmly. 'Has Iain been telling you what's happening here?'

'Aye, he has that.' Geordie was polite but didn't smile.

Dad told him more of the details about the deer farm and the other plans, but still Geordie's face remained expressionless.

'I tell you what I wanted to ask you,' Mr Barlass continued. 'Your ancestors lived in this glen. Don't you think it'd be only right if your people had a place in the glen as it's going to be?'

At these words, a wonderful, radiant smile broke across Geordie's face, lighting up his big dark eyes and crinkling his cheeks. He grasped Iain's father's hand in a grip that made him wince.

'God bliss me!' he roared. 'Ye're a real gentleman! Ye're bien hantle richt enough!'

'You're a gentleman yourself,' said Mr Barlass, 'to have been so good to Iain and to have carried on your way of life in such a decent way. You'll always be welcome here – after all, it's your home.'

Geordie smiled again. 'I just hope ye'll get ither fowk tae think the same wey,' he said.

Councillor Wilson stepped forward and held out his hand to Geordie. 'Well, I will anyhow,' he assured him, 'and I'll argue your case in the Council, I promise you. There'll be those who'll oppose it, but I think we can beat them.'

'There'll be building work available,' said Mr Christie, 'if you've some strong men to do it.'

'Dinna fash yersel aboot that,' Geordie answered. 'Me and ma faimily'll gie ye plenty o wark.'

'That's not all,' said Dad. 'Lots of people will come to see where the treasure was found, so we'll need a piper on the rock.'

'Jist whit I was thinkin masel,' said Geordie. 'And wha better than me, Geordie Mac an Dhu?'

Iain was delighted to hear Geordie go back to the Gaelic form of his name, now that the curse had been lifted.

'What about the silver?' asked Fattie. 'Where did they get the silver they used to make the ornaments?'

'Ah,' said Geordie, 'they jist melted doon auld yins. I dinny ken o ony ither wey o gettin it.'

'No silver mines?'

'I dinna think so. Nae here onywey.'

'Never mind,' said Councillor Wilson, 'we've made a start to something that's going to be a great undertaking.'

Everyone seemed in a mood to celebrate and soon they were all sharing a picnic of coffee and sandwiches, sitting around on the grass, on mossy stones or in sheltered nooks.

'Please give us another tune on your pipes, Geordie,' suggested Dad. 'This is the ideal place to listen to them.'

So Geordie lifted his pipes to his shoulder and started to play again. Everyone just sat there in the sun, enjoying the sound and the beauty of the hills. Iain felt at last that the dream of Seamas Dhu had come true and *Gleann a' Chadail* had begun to waken up from its long sleep.

Glossary

aathin	*Scots* everything
amadan mor	*Gaelic* great fool
beag	*Gaelic* small
bourtree	*Scots* elder tree
brochan	*Gaelic* gruel, thin oatmeal porridge
country hantle	*cant* non-travellers
een	*Scots* eyes
feartie	*Scots* coward
feck	*cant* give
gille, ghille	*Gaelic* boy
haar	*Scots* cold mist
heather cowe	*Scots* clump of heather
linn	*Scots* waterfall
lour	*cant* money
mang the cant	*cant* speak the travellers' code language
mor	*Gaelic* big
peevie	*cant* drunk
ruadh	*Gaelic* red-haired
stravaigin	*Scots* wandering

Other titles available from

SCOTTISH CHILDREN'S PRESS

An A–Z of Scots Words for young readers
1 899827 03 X

Aiken Drum: a story in Scots for young readers
Anne Forsyth; illustrated by Dianne Sutherland; 1 899827 00 5

Classic Children's Games from Scotland
Kendric Ross; illustrated by John MacKay; 1 899827 12 9

Kitty Bairdie: a story in Scots for young readers
Anne Forsyth; illustrated by Dianne Sutherland; 1 899827 01 3

Little Kirstie of Aberlour
Samantha Valentine; illustrated by Vikki Petrie; 1 899827 13 7

A Richt Cuddy and ither Fables
William J. Rae; illustrated by Norman Glen; 1 899827 02 1

Strathclyde Bairns: new writing from Scotland's children
1 899827 20 X

Teach the Bairns to Bake: Traditional Scottish Baking for Beginners
Liz Ashworth; 1 899827 24 2

Teach the Bairns to Cook: Traditional Scottish Recipes for Beginners
Liz Ashworth; 1 899827 23 4

Touching the Past: Archaeology 5–14
Neil and Elizabeth Curtis (ed.); 1 899827 63 3

Wallace, Bruce, and the War of Independence
Antony Kamm; illustrated by Jennifer Campbell; 1 899827 15 3

Wee Willie Winkie and other rhymes for Scots children
Fiona Petersen (ed.); 1 899827 17 X

The Wild Haggis an the Greetin-faced Nyaff
Stuart McHardy; illustrated by Alistair Phimister; 1 899827 04 8